I Am Her THE MISTRESS

V. BROWN

STREET CHRONICLES

Published by:
G Street Chronicles
P.O. Box 1822
Jonesboro, GA 30237-1822

www.gstreetchronicles.com
fans@gstreetchronicles.com

Cover design: Hot Book Covers, www.hotbookcovers.com

Cover model: Valia Brown

ISBN 13: 978-1-9384426-9-8´
ISBN 10: 1938442695
LCCN: 2013931245

Join us on our social networks
G Street Chronicles Fan Page
G Street Chronicles CEO Exclusive Readers Group

Follow us on Twitter
@GStreetChronicl

Acknowledgements

First and foremost I want to thank God for blessing me with the gift to tell stories that may either take a person out of a bad mood or touch a person in more ways than one.

I would like to acknowledge my mother Vadia and my father Theodore aka Ted. Though we might not always see eye to eye I thank you for being there the times you are. I love you both!

I want to thank my sisters Vatia, Tamara aka Bam, Marquessa and Marquetta for supporting and encouraging me when I felt I didn't have any support.

Thank you to my brothers Lorenzo, Michael, Ted Jr. Courtney, Aj and my nephews Jarvis Jr. aka Mook, Lil Zo and Zion—you give me the strength to keep pushing.

To my godmother Dot for being the one person who always believed in me. You always tell me how proud you are of me and I appreciate that. You don't know how much that means to hear it.

Thank you to all of my aunts, uncles and cousins. When I need family I smile because I can count on y'all in one way or another.

Thank you to all of my close "Real" friends who keep it real with me. Y'all do more for me then y'all can imagine. If you're questioning if you're in this category that means you're not because my real friends would never question it. To my friends who supported my first 2 books by 1-clicking them and turning around and purchasing an autographed copy, y'all are the best. Stay on this journey with me…I love y'all.

I want to acknowledge a good friend of mine Renee, whose middle name is Lorraine, which is where one of the character's names came from. I ran the idea of this book by her and she loved it. She actually pushed me to write it in the beginning because

I was apprehensive. I also want to thank her daughter, who is my goddaughter Tyquasia. She asked me if I would use her name in one of my books and it was only right that I did. This is the one.

What would I do without my FLATS?! Qiona aka Blaque, Chandra aka BG & Chanda aka Chan. You ladies are the best! You're like the sorority sisters I wanted, but never got the chance to have. I can come to y'all with anything good, bad or indifferent and you never judge me and always understand. I love y'all for that.

To all of my readers who 1-clicked my first book Broken Promise and the sequel Black Ice, not knowing me from a can of paint, but you were willing to take a chance on me and my stories—for that I say Thank You. Your support means the world.

To the Facebook groups that I'm a part of, starting with The G Street Chronicles CEO Exclusive Readers Group! Divas and Goons I love y'all because y'all go so hard in pushing me to keep that heat coming. My Urban Book Club and My Urban Books Blog. Kindle Reading Club, Black Faithful Sisters and Brothers Book Club, United Sisters Bookclub, Let's Talk Relationships & Books!!! Y'all all show me a lot of love and any book club that I didn't mention I apologize, but thank you as well.

Last, but definitely never least, Thank You to the company and people behind the company that made it all possible, y'all made my dream a reality. G Street Chronicles CEO George Sherman Hudson and COO Shawna A., I'm rocking with y'all while we float to the top past all the naysayers. We are definitely more than just a publishing company, we are a family and I wouldn't want to be a part of any other family. #GStreet

To everyone who was mentioned know that you are near and dear to my heart. Thank you and I love you. Alright now…let's get on to this juiciness. I know you can't wait to begin reading. Enjoy!

-V. Brown

Prologue

A nother night of passionate love making to a man who wasn't her man; but was she wrong for feeling like he was? Who would've ever thought Tyquasia Roberts could or would be a mistress? The things he did to her, the way he made her feel, were all parts of her decision to openly acknowledge herself as a mistress—his mistress. She sat there daydreaming about her night filled with ecstasy. It couldn't be described as anything other than pure passion that ended in an abrupt halt.

"I wish we didn't always have to come to my place to spend time together. It would be nice to go over to your house sometimes so I can get a feel for how you like to live."

"What did I tell you about talking like that? In due time, you know that now isn't the right time for me to be making those kinds of moves. Let's just sit back, relax and enjoy each other while we have the time to," Nasir *replied, checking his watch for the second time since he'd gotten there.*

"What are you checking your watch for? You know she'll be heading out of town on one of her gigs that she has in another state—those bullshit trips she's always taking. I hate bringing her up, but if you're that in a rush to get back to her maybe you should do like a good little doggy and go on back

home," Tyquasia challenged.

"Shh, stop all that! Is it really necessary for you to go there? You hate bringing her up—well then don't. Come on over here, I got something that'll take your mind off of all that dumb shit."

Tyquasia perked up a little. She knew that she was being hard on him, but she had to; otherwise, he would probably take her for a joke and think that what they were doing would always be an option for him to use at will. In her mind, she was making it clear to Nasir that it wasn't.

"You knew that I was coming over, so you should've answered the door ready for me. Isn't that what you texted me earlier when I was in my meeting? I think your words were that you were ready for me to take control. You wanted to feel your body become one with mine like it did the first time. Yeah, that's what you said and now I'm here to make it happen." Nasir said pulling the zipper down in the back of her dress; exposing her bare, smooth back.

One kiss after another, leading a trail down to the small of her back, he slid her dress off, only to reveal that Tyquasia wasn't wearing any panties.

"I guess you were kinda ready for me huh?" he joked. Nasir dropped to his knees and parted her ass cheeks which faced him, and with precision, he began a dance with her pearl that he sucked from its hiding spot.

Tyquasia enjoyed every minute of it. Her juices ran freely as her body reacted to his touch. Nasir was a man of many talents and pleasing a woman had to be at the top of the list.

He slid from under her, picked her up in the air and she wrapped her legs around his waist as he backed her up to the wall. In one swift motion, he unbuttoned his pants and dropped them and his boxers to the floor; teasing her, he massaged his head against her opening—around and around he went, never going in. Those were the types of mind tricks he played on her which drove her wild.

After a few seconds of sexually stringing her along, Nasir lay her gently on the bed and eased his way in, settling her nerves a bit before he took her on the ride of her life. What he was doing to her could only be described as sitting on top of a jack rabbit as it drilled deeply into concrete. Best feeling in the world, she thought.

When their sexcapade was over and they were both exhausted, each wanting to continue but neither making the move, Nasir's phone alerted him to an incoming text message. He picked up his phone and glared at the time and then down again at the text which was from his wife asking was he ok. He hopped off the bed and began to get dressed.

Tyquasia sat up and shook her head.

"Not now Tyquasia. I will make this up to you. I didn't know it was so late. What business meeting do you know of that takes place at two o'clock in the morning? I need to get going. I'll see you tomorrow; I can take you out to lunch while you have a break between classes or something. But right now, I have to go," he said kissing her lips as he slid on his shirt.

"You know that this has got to stop Nasir. I can't keep going on like this!" Tyquasia yelled as Nasir exited her room.

"I know, and it will stop; just give me some time to work things out. It's all a matter of time," he replied before leaving out her front door.

Tyquasia just sunk back into her sheets, wrapping up in them to feel like she was being held by him. Same shit, different day. Damn, she thought.

"Hey Ty, what's on your mind, you seemed distant in class today?" Paige asked as she walked up and sat down with her lunch.

"Girl, a lot. I've been sitting here thinking and asking myself the same question over and over again. "Do you think you could ever be the mistress of a man who probably won't ever leave his wife?" Tyquasia lowered her head, avoiding eye contact while sitting in the break area for lunch before her next class. She had asked herself that very question for several months; this time she wanted a point of view that was different from her own.

"Not this shit again girl! First of all I wouldn't ever be a man's mistress. If I can't be the 'one and only' then I don't want to be any. I know you're not still messing with Nasir are you? I thought you nipped that relationship in the bud when he told you he didn't know how to just leave his wife—which sounded like a bunch of bull shit to me I might add," Paige said chastising her best friend.

Tyquasia got quiet and put her head down, not really embarrassed by Paige's remark, but trying to hide the grin slowly appearing on her face.

"Girl, I don't know what your problem is, that nigga is fine as fuck! Six foot three, Black and Cuban mixed, solid build, with that almond-colored skin...mmm," she said licking her lips obviously reminiscing. "That low cut fits him so right; pearly white teeth and his whole 80's tailored-made swag just turns me on. I can't get enough of him. He's a beast in the bedroom. You remember how I used to brag about Benzino's shit? Nasir runs circles around him in the bedroom."

Paige shook her head. "Look at us," she said as she stood

up pulling Tyquasia up with her. "We're two bad ass bitches! I don't mean to toot my own horn, but these killer curves ain't nothing to be fucked with. Yeah, I'm a full-figured, voluptuous woman. Standing 5'9" inches tall and weighing in at 170 pounds—I hold my weight just fine. These blue eyes make dudes never tell a lie. The double D's and phat ass are just added incentives. Unlike most white women, my lips are full and I wear these extensions because it makes me happy, not because some man asked me to. The chocolate brothers love all of this, and I'm sure the caramel and light-skin men that you like, love all of you too. I never understood your attraction for the light meat. I want a Tyrese-looking man; single, trusting, loving, a good heart, an amazing sex game and all that jazz. But I be damned if I will settle for a married man just because he fucks me right; and you shouldn't either."

Tyquasia looked at herself from head to toe; examining each part carefully. "We are some bad asses that's for damn sure; 'cause I know this mocha smooth skin of mine and these slanted hazel eyes make the niggas drool. At twenty-two years old, you can tell I will age just fine and that's a sign that I keep the stress and drama out of my life. Shit… good sex only makes it all better. I've grown to have strong feelings for Nasir and I think he's grown feelings for me too. I just don't know if he's ready to let that model—perfect in everybody's eyes—wife of his go. I'm not settling—just trying to see where things go."

Unlike Paige, Tyquasia really didn't have to make it known to others how fly she was. It was recognized without prompting on her part and showed on everyone's face when she stepped into a room. Although she'd grown up in the

Pork 'n' Bean Projects in Miami, Florida, her mother tried her best to shelter Tyquasia from the streets and the mentality that often went along with it. She didn't allow Tyquasia to run the streets or fuck a bunch of different dudes like all her friends were doing. Her mother made her focus on school and Tyquasia did just that until she hit seventeen and met and fell in love with a street hustler named Benzino who ran her block. That's kind of where the change came in, and now here she was growing into the woman she'd become.

"Suit yourself BFF, just don't come running back to me when he breaks your heart and tells you he wants to work things out with his wife and the only way he can do that is to leave you alone and focus on *their* relationship. I've seen the shit happen too many times on the soaps and in a lot of my favorite movies," Paige said sitting back down to finish her lunch.

"I got this one; just trust me. I've thought this all the way out," Tyquasia said with a wicked smile.

"Ahh shit! I don't want no part of this 'cause I already know when you have a plan…there's trouble in paradise. Let's head on over to our next class, you know professor Alexandra hates when we're late."

Chapter One
Meet Tyquasia

This change of life all started with Tyquasia "Ty" Roberts when she was a seventeen-year-old, over-protected teenager. The only time she had to herself was when she walked to and from school since her mother was so over protective. Ty wasn't allowed many phone calls or friends to come over and hang out, her days were filled with school, homework and house chores. She lived in Liberty Square Housing, aka the Pork 'n' Beans in Miami, Florida.

One day on her stroll home from school she saw the man she'd been fantasying about every night before she went to sleep. There he was sitting out front of the bodega in his 2010 Maybach looking fine as ever; but just like any other day, Tyquasia admired him from a far and kept it moving. She was a block away from the projects and only a couple of steps passed his car when he beeped his horn.

"Aye Shawty, let me holla at you for a minute," Benzino said stepping out of his car. He was dressed in all black, his signature color. He was a chocolate brother with smooth skin and his hair was cut in a bald fade. Benzino stood 6'6" and weighed about 220 pounds. His eyes were dark like they'd witnessed things in life that no one should ever have to. Bottom line was that Benzino was a sexy gangsta brother if ever there was one.

Tyquasia stopped in her tracks looking around to make sure that he was talking to her. When she realized he was, she calmly turned around keeping a straight face. "My name isn't Shawty," she said, placing her hand on her hip while adding much attitude like she'd seen her friend Khia do when a dude tried to get at her. It was a sign just to let him know that she wasn't like all the other girls in the hood who got weak in the knees at the thought of him possibly talking to them.

"My bad, what is your name ma? I see you walking past here a lot, but you never speak to anyone. You ain't too friendly, I like that," Benzino said.

"My name is Tyquasia, but my friends call me Ty. I've been told it's not good to be too friendly. I see you from time to time when I walk down this block too. Your name is Benzino right?" Tyquasia asked.

"Since I wanna be your friend too, I'm gonna call you Ty also. I see you've heard of me."

"That's cool. I may not hang out in the streets, but the streets are always talking and a lot of the dudes at my school brag about you. 'Oh, Benzino—that dude in the streets—can't nobody move weight around here without going through Benzino.' Them lil' niggas talk about you like you're some type of god," Tyquasia said laughing at her own statement.

"Oh yeah? I think them lil' niggas run they mouth too much, but as long as they recognize what's real it's all good. Look, I wanted to get at you 'cause I like your style. You're not like these ghetto birds out here. You're focused, smart, and I'm sure sexy with a little dressing up. How old are you anyway? I'm not trying to do no time behind yo' ass."

Tyquasia looked at her clothes and shoes. No, she wasn't

rockin' the latest trends, but she managed with the knock offs that she had. She knew if she ever got her hands on some cash she would get all the flyest shit, top brands, and the baddest heels available. But for now, she was just settling for what she had. The first opportunity she got, she planned on showing off all the growth her body had gone through in the last couple of years. She was filling out just fine. A body that matched her beautiful face was all the ammo she needed to get the ballers.

"You like my style huh? Well, sorry to disappoint you Benzino, but I'm only seventeen. I still have a good five and a half months before my eighteenth birthday," Tyquasia said hating her age. *Damn, I should've lied to this nigga and told his ass that I just turned eighteen. Fuck!* she thought as she cursed at herself.

A dude named Rex stumbled out the front door of the bodega. You could tell he wasn't a crackhead, but he was definitely on some type of drugs. His swag was tight and his shoes fresh to death, but his movements and the way he acted was suspect.

Benzino had obviously noticed the same thing as Rex came out. "Hold that thought for a minute sweetheart; I need to go see a man about a horse," he turned and headed over to the front of the bodega.

Tyquasia knew she should've just headed home, but she was nosey and wanted to see what was going to transpire so she stayed put and watched the scene unfold.

Rex was leaned up against the wall playing a scratch off, alone and carrying on a conversation by himself when Benzino approached him. He didn't know who had walked up on him until he felt the force of the butt of a handgun crash down on his temple. With one blow Rex was knocked to the ground; damn near incoherent.

"If I have to do every one of you lil' muthafuckas like this to teach y'all some respect, I will. Now where the fuck is my money? You been duckin' and dodging Allure like crazy, so now I gotta sit on the block and find you my damn self. Yo' ass better have some good shit to say," Benzino snapped, gun cocked and pointed straight at Rex's head.

"Ma…Ma…man don't do me like that, you know I'm good for it. I just got caught up in some shit. I'm gone get you your money," Rex replied terrified as he felt the blood running from the side of his head.

"I know damn right you gone give me my money. I don't even know why my nigga trusted you to be on the team in the first place. I had already peeped game, I saw that you weren't built for this kind of life. Now look at you…you smoking, snorting or shootin' up that shit; which one is it? Don't lie nigga cause I know you're doing one of those. You can see it all over your face. Look at yo' lips, all cracked and the skin's peeling off. It don't take an Einstein to see what time it is with you."

"I only tried the shit one time; I swear man. It was on some dumb ass 'Truth or Dare' shit," he said scratching himself like crazy.

Benzino had heard enough, but instead of killing Rex, he decided to stomp him until he felt he was near death and then he would let his addiction kill him instead. Benzino put in work over time, punching and kicking Rex wherever he could land them. When he saw that Rex was no longer moving, but still breathing, Benzino checked himself and brushed over his clothes to knock any wrinkles that he might've gotten from the work he'd just put in. After doing so, he walked back over to Ty.

"Sorry about that, but I gotta put in work from time to time. Where were we? Oh yeah, five and half months you say? Ok, that's all the time we need to get to know each other inside and out. Hop in, I'm gonna drop you off at your house. Lock your number in my phone so that we can get up with each other sometime tomorrow after I finish handling some business," Benzino said handing Ty his iPhone.

* * * * *

From the day Ty gave Benzino her number they were inseparable. There wasn't a day that went by where one was seen without the other. Benzino would pick Ty up in the morning and take her to school every day and when it was time for school to let out, Benzino was there to pick his shawty up. He even let her ride with him on some of his jobs; whether he was collecting the cash count for that week, or checking up on a spot, Ty was with Benzino as he did his business.

She wondered why he was always the one doing the money pickup, especially seeing as though he was the boss. She figured he would have someone else from his team doing all that. Benzino broke it down to her one day and he told her he wasn't like the niggas she saw in the movies; he preferred to be hands on in every aspect of his business. He said the game was his lively hood, and he couldn't afford to leave it all up to the next nigga to see that shit was running right. So when it came to running things, if it wasn't Benzino running his business, it was his right hand man, Allure, handling the shit. No other hands touched his shit. That was as far as his trust in another nigga went.

As promised, once the five and half months were over and it was Tyquasia's eighteenth birthday, Benzino officially made her his girl. He threw her a surprise birthday party and invited some her friends. After the party was over, they headed back to one of the three homes that he owned, but rarely stayed in. She felt like she was in a mansion. Benzino led her to the master bedroom where he began to teach her the beauty of full sex. Yeah, they had done the oral sex thing throughout the time they were getting to know each other, but he had never penetrated her. They never went all the way, but the oral sex was off the chain. Ty thought sex couldn't get any better than what she felt when she came for the first time from the way he worked his tongue. He told her how he preferred his dick sucked, and he made sure she knew to keep her teeth out of the way, keep her mouth really wet, and never choke. *Relax your throat,* he would say. Those were the instructions he gave her concerning oral sex; but now she was being taught new lessons—lessons on making love.

From the first time she saw his pole, all she could think about was the length and width of what he was working with. *Was that supposed to go in her forbidden fruit? Could she take it all?* Shoot this was all new to her; she was still a virgin and when Benzino found that out he knew the wait was well worth it.

He climbed on top of her and spread her thick thighs; getting her into the missionary position. Although it was one of his least favorite positions he felt that he should start off with it since it was her first time. He grabbed his gloved manhood and slowly penetrated her—making sure to take it easy.

"This is just like your throat ma, relax your muscles and once I'm fully in, contract your muscles around me." He opted not to put his full ten and half inch dick in her at one time, and when he was midway in, he began to pump slowly.

Tyquasia's face went from one of pain to one of sheer pleasure. She was really starting to get into the rhythm. When Benzino felt like she was comfortable, he rolled onto his back keeping himself inside of her. "I want you to ride me baby. I'll guide you," he said as he rubbed along the sides of her hips.

Ty wasn't hearing that though; she was feeling the three glasses of Ciroc that she'd had at her party and felt like she could ride him without any help. She lifted herself up some and glided back down on his dick taking another inch in. Every time she did that, another inch went deep inside her until she had the full ten and half inches inside her. She began to ride him, holding on to the head board just in front of her. Benzino cuffed her ass. She pulled up, leaving just the head in the entrance of her soaking wet pussy; then she slid back down at the same time, squeezing her pussy muscles with each movement which sent Benzino into a frenzy.

Never before had he had any female ride him like that in his whole twenty-five years of existence and he'd been getting it in since he was a jitt; so he'd had his share. They sped up their rhythm after another ten minutes passed of sweaty, hot, steamy sex; Benzino felt the head of his dick swell.

"Ahh fuck, I'm 'bout to bust!"

"Hold that shit baby. I'm right behind you," Ty said as she felt Benzino hold on tight to her waist and give her long, hard strokes. Their bodies began to shiver at the same time;

bringing each other to a sexual high like none other.

* * * * *

Tyquasia graduated from high school shortly after her eighteenth birthday. Her plan was to go to a nursing school that was only a couple of hours away from Miami in Orlando, Florida; but Benzino wasn't having that at all. He told her he didn't want her going to school or working. He'd become obsessed, possessive and overbearing. He wanted her around him at all times. She felt like she was going to go crazy. To any regular, around the way girl with no dreams or goals, the attention she was receiving would be viewed with them thinking Ty was living the golden life; but Ty didn't see it that way. In her mind, she was only living a life of imprisonment; and she hated it.

Three years of dating, sexing, being cooped up in a mansion not able to do anything except get her hair, nails, and feet done and shopping, quickly became Ty's reality. She felt drained and just wanted an outlet. Waking up every day feeling like her life was worthless, she would often think about what her mother told her before she moved out of her house, "You're making a big mistake, and you're going to end up being a pregnant nobody who has to depend on a man to take care of her. I want more for you than that; but you're grown now and I can't continue to make decisions for you. You will learn from your mistakes."

Ty was happy that she hadn't been pregnant once during their time together, but she figured that with the help of secretly taking birth control, she didn't have anything to worry about. Every time they had sex, Benzino would purposely not use a condom and let off all his seed into her so that he could get her pregnant and have an even tighter hold on her life; but she wasn't having it. Ty never missed not even one day of taking her birth control.

It was only a matter of time before Ty started telling Benzino she was going one place and she would end up at another. The lies started rolling off her tongue with so much ease that she began to believe them herself. If she had to be sneaky to have a little fun…she would. When it came down to it, Tyquasia didn't have anything except the things that Benzino gave her, and she knew that if there ever came a time where he didn't want her around anymore, she would be left high and dry with nothing. That thought wasn't sitting too well with her, so something had to change and fast.

Tyquasia got her wish one day while relaxing by the pool, listening to music by Monica. Her cell phone began to ring. *I bet this ain't nobody but Benzino wanting to know what's for dinner. Fuck that! I'm not cooking tonight. I'm tired of cooking, cleaning, and playing housewife without the ring or the title,* Ty thought as she picked her Android up from the table next to her.

"Hey D, what's up?" Ty asked after seeing the name scroll across the screen of her phone.

"Ain't shit ma; I'm about to head back home. Atlanta treated me real right though, I must say. I know you don't really want to be hearing this right now, but I was riding through Bankhead and saw ya man's car surrounded by a couple of them blue boy's cars. I don't know what was up with that, but he wasn't in his car so you might want to call and check up on him," D suggested.

"Thanks for the heads up. I don't know what this nigga done gone and got himself caught up in this time. Hit me up when you land and get settled in. I'm going to call Benz and see what's going on with him," Ty said.

"No problem. Ok, I'll do that. You be easy; whatever that dumb ass nigga done got himself caught up in shouldn't stress you out. This might be just what you need," D replied.

"Yeah, we'll see," Tyquasia sighed heavily. She ended the call and immediately scrolled through her phone to find Benz's number. She clicked on it and placed the phone up to her ear. The line rang once and went straight to voicemail. *I know this nigga ain't forwardin' my call when I'm trying to check up on his ass,* Ty thought. She tried to call him again with no answer. *Damn, I hope the cops haven't arrested him. I know he carries that fuckin' piece on him. Let me just think positive,* she thought.

Ty got up and headed in the house; her little relaxation moment was over and it was time for her to get on her *wifey* shit. She took a shower and while she was throwing on some clothes her phone began to ring. *Unknown name, unknown number? I wonder who this could be,* Ty thought reading the caller I.D.

When she slid talk button on the screen, an automated voice came on, "You have a collect call from inmate…'It's me' a voice cut in and said…in a correctional facility. To accept the call press one; to block all calls from. . ." Ty pressed one not needing to hear the rest of the options.

"Baby, what the hell happened?" Ty asked trying to sound concerned.

"To tell you the truth, I don't know what happened. The shit was crazy, ya heard me? Ain't too much talkin' I'm gone do over this phone though, I've already talked to Chris and he's tryna see what's going on. He should be comin' to visit me in a few," Benzino said sounding calm like he wasn't even locked up.

"What are they trying to charge you with? Are they keeping you over night? What can I do to help you and to help myself stay sane?" Ty asked rattling off a bunch of questions.

"I don't want you worrying' that pretty little head of yours. I'm good. If I'm staying overnight I'll set you up a visitation for tomorrow around seven at night," Benzino said not really meaning it. There was no way he wanted Ty seeing him in that light. "Chris will be by after his visitation with me to explain everything to you."

The automated voice came on again, "You have one minute left."

"Damn! Already? It doesn't even seem like we've been on the phone for ten minutes. Ugh!" Ty replied to the warning.

"Shit! You heard everything I said right? He'll be by there with further instructions and information from me. I love you Ty and don't worry about..."

"Your time is up! Good bye," the automated voice said.

A smile crept across Tyquasia's face. For the first time in three years she had a night to herself and she was definitely going to take advantage of it. Hell, who knew when she would get another chance like this again. Ty picked up her phone and dialed Khia's number. Khia grew up around the same neighborhood as Tyquasia and she was one of the only chicks from around their way that actually talked to Ty when they were in school.

"What's the T bitch?" Khia said smacking on something extra loud.

Khia is a ghetto, dark-skinned, short—only standing 5'5" and weighing 140 pounds—hood chick. She wasn't the cutest girl in the bunch, but most dudes called her *fuckable*. Ty overlooked all of that because Khia befriended her when not too many other chicks would even look her way. Khia didn't have the best reputation in the hood seeing that any dude that paid her the smallest amount of attention, she ended up having sex with on the first day; no matter where they were.

"Nothing! Girl, I was calling to see what you were getting into tonight? I'm trying to go out, have some drinks, and dance until I can't dance anymore. Are you down?" Ty asked.

"Ty you know damn well I ain't got no money or nothing to wear. How the hell am I going to go somewhere?" Khia replied continuing to smack what sounded like some juicy gum.

"I forgot to mention it's a night out on me. I'll bring over one of my new outfits that I haven't even taken out of the bag yet. What happened to the job you got at McDonald's a couple of weeks ago?" Ty asked.

"If you call me more often, instead of being stuck under that fine ass Benzino, you would know that those fuckers fired me; talkin' bout my drawer came up short too many days in a row. They also told me not to worry about picking up my check seeing as though I had only worked five days and the amount the drawer came up short was equal to what my check would be. They said as far as they were concerned, I wouldn't have a check to pick up and we could call it even," Khia said.

"First of all, keep yo' eyes off my man. And secondly, I know you weren't in those people's place stealing from them Khia! You know what...don't even answer that. Knowing you, you probably were taking twenty and fifty dollars here and there thinking they weren't going to miss the money or catch you doing it. I don't know what I'm gone do with your ass. Just be out the shower and ready to throw the outfit on when I get there," Ty stated.

"Yeah bitch, I was stealing; 'cause everybody ain't got a man who will swoop in and take them out the projects, pay all their bills and only expect them to play wifey at home in return like you do." I swear I only deal with this cocky bitch *'cause I can freeload off her ass whenever she does decide to come around,* Khia thought from her end of the phone line.

"Yeah, whatever. Bring me some heels to match the outfit too. See ya soon," Khia said and then hung up.

Tyquasia hurried to her closet. It was after ten at night, and since she hadn't planned on going out, it would take her a little while to find something to wear. *Maybe I should think about what I'm going to wear while I do my makeup,* Ty thought. It was 10:50 p.m. by the time she finished her makeup and finally figured out what she wanted to wear. She slid into a fire red Bodycon skirt and opted for a black and white stripped sheer long sleeve tunic top. Instead of buttoning it all the way to the top, she decided to leave a little cleavage showing so the top three buttons went unbuttoned. Her shoes were what inspired the outfit. They were the newly released stripped Louis Vuitton pumps. Her hair was done in a high bun with a swoop bang. She was definitely feeling herself as she looked in the tall wide mirror that took up one whole wall in the master bedroom. She puckered up her lips as if she was about to kiss someone—admiring her flawless makeup and the red Ruby Kisses lipstick that glistened smoothly on her lips.

"Damn, I'm a bad bitch!" Ty said out loud. *I better get*

going, it's getting kind of late. I want us to make an entrance before everybody starts getting drunk, Ty thought. She grabbed her key, her purse and the bag containing the pink BeBe dress and cream colored pumps that Khia was going to wear, and she left the house; totally forgetting about Chris coming to talk to her about Benzino's situation.

Twenty minutes later Tyquasia was at Khia's apartment in the Pork 'n' Beans. As soon as Khia opened the door she started in, "Damn, look at you all dressed up and shit. Where we going, 'cause you're snatched to the gods honey. How much all that shit you got on cost? I bet too damn much. Let me see what you brought me to wear," Khia said holding her hand out.

"Why are you always worrying about how much this and that cost? This stuff ain't nothing but materialistic shit. At the end of the day, I'd rather have a career doing something I love and financing my damn self. Now what I brought you is hot, so I don't want to hear your damn mouth about it not showing enough tits, it not being short enough, or whatever other negative shit that comes to your mind," Ty said handing Khia the bag.

Khia quickly opened it and pulled out the contents. "Ok, ok…I'm diggin' these heels; but I don't know about this dress. It might be too long fareal since I'm so short. Seems like this is for tall people like yourself…you know what I mean. I'm going to see though…it might fit right," Khia said walking off. Before she left the room completely she said over her shoulder, "I worry about money 'cause I ain't got none. I'm stuck in the same hell hole I grew up in. It's kinda like the cycle repeating itself. My mother lived here and now I have my own place here. You're crazy as fuck if you don't chill out and just let that man of yours continue to take care of yo' ass as you sit up there not having to do shit. That career you want so bad can wait; right now you need to enjoy what you got."

Little do you know, my nigga that you claim is so good to me might not be around for God knows how long. I have to think about me, my future and decide what career I want to work in for the rest of my life. Ty wanted to say, but she opted not to even reply, seeing as though she and Khia had had this same conversation numerous times since she'd begun her relationship with Benzino. She already knew what it would lead to.

When Khia walked out from her bedroom into the living room, the dress she had taken back with her looked completely different. She had clearly taken some scissors to the dress because the bottom, which should have reached her knees, was now cut an inch under her ass cheeks. There were slits going up both sides of the dress.

"That's what took you fifteen minutes to do? You were back there cutting up everything but the BeBe logo off of the dress. Let's go! It's 11:30 and it's going to take us a minute to get there through Miami's traffic," Ty said walking out the front door.

"You know how I do. The dress was cute and all, but it wasn't my style; now this here is bussin'," Khia said.

"If you mean 'busted,' I agree." Tyquasia whispered under her breath as she hit the unlock button on her key chain.

"Did you say something?" Khia asked.

"What? Girl you're hearing things. Come on…hop in," Ty lied.

I could've sworn I heard this bitch say something, Khia

thought as she got in the car.

"So where are we shakin' our asses at tonight? I'm tryna get fucked up and go home with somebody's baller man," Khia said smacking on her gum.

"Why are you smacking on that gum like that? You know I don't get out like that so I was just gonna ride down to South Beach and see what's poppin'. Anyway…you're the party animal; you tell me what's jumpin' tonight. You talking about getting somebody's man, don't have us fighting some bitches 'cause you wanna get fresh with somebody's man," Ty replied.

"I can't help it, if I don't chew this gum like this, I will grind my teeth down to nubs. I popped a Molly. I heard them cash money dudes supposed to be partying at LIV tonight. That's down on Collins Avenue in South Beach. If them hoes don't want their men taken tonight they better stay home 'cause we outchea," Khia stated.

"LIV it is then. Let me warn you now, just because I'm going out doesn't mean I don't still have a man. I just want to have a little fun that's all," Ty said making it known what her intentions were.

Surprisingly, Khia didn't have a comeback to Tyquasia's remark.

They arrived at LIV in no time at all thanks to Ty being behind the wheel. After handing over her keys and a hefty tip to the valet, they walked through the lobby and got in the VIP line.

"Now, you know damn well we ain't on the list, so why are we about to waste time standing over here?" Khia said switching her weight from side to side.

"If you shut up for a hot second, you would see that I have

a plan. Do you see that general admission so-called line over there? I'm not standing in that crowd for two hours hoping to get in. Money talks; now watch me work," Ty said checking herself out to make sure everything was in place.

"For some reason you always seem to bring that goon out that you so secretly keep stashed away. Yo' ass should've been a part of the *goon squad* when we were in school," Khia joked.

Ty had to laugh at Khia's joke, it was true she called herself a *diva,* but she had some goon tendencies. When the line finally reached Ty and Khia the bouncer looked them over, looked away and then placed his eyes on Ty. "Name?" he asked.

"Well, I'm Tyquasia and this is my friend Khia."

He looked over the two pages of names he had in his hand. "Nope, I don't have a Tyquasia or Khia; sorry mami. You can step to the side."

"Ok listen, I know our name isn't on the list, but you see that crowd over there gathered around the general admission door? My girl and I aren't trying to stand in that line all night. What do we have to do to get up in this place?" Ty asked.

He looked around again and stated flatly, "That'll be a hundred a piece and I'll take your number."

Ty looked at him with a blank stare, pulled out two hundred dollar bills from her clutch and handed it to him. "Make that a hundred a piece and no number," Tyquasia said.

"Have it your way then sexy mami," he replied moving to the side to allow them entry.

"You could've had *my* number papi, but you were checking out the wrong chick," Khia said rubbing her phat ass up against him as she walked past.

"I wonder if YMCMB is here yet. I sho' wouldn't mind getting a room with Birdman and Wayne. Shit…I can rub on Birdman's bald head while he tickles my cat and Wayne can get some of the world's best dome. Super Head ain't got shit on me!" Khia yelled so that Ty could hear her over the music.

"As loud as you just yelled that, I'm sure them Young Money Cash Money Ballers and everybody else in here heard what you said. I just want to get my drink on. What do you want to drink? I'm buying a bottle!" Ty yelled as she made her way to an area that overlooked damn near the whole club. People were all over the dance floor enjoying themselves.

"Where the hell is the waitress? I'm ready to pop a bottle," Ty yelled scanning the VIP area.

"I think I see one coming up the stairs; I'll be right back." Khia said twisting off in the direction of the stairs—dress rising with each step.

Tyquasia sat back and enjoyed the ambiance of the club. She looked back towards the stairs to see where Khia had gone and there he was. When he reached the top step, their eyes met. It seemed as though the music stopped playing and the only people there were the two of them.

Damn, who the fuck is that? Ty wondered.

Her eyes wandered his six three, solid-built frame. His almond skin looked smooth as butter under the low club lights. The low haircut with semi waves fit him just right. Everything about him read *grown ass man*. His style was 80's with a tailor-made flare. When he began to walk closer to Ty she noticed his ice. In his right ear was a Canadian black diamond stud cut earring. Around his neck lay an eighteen inch black diamond encrusted chain with a cross medallion.

Setting it off on his wrist was a black-on-black Geneva watch. The last thing Ty saw before the sexy hunk was in her space, was a wedding band blingin' on his ring finger.

Fuck! I just studied this dude from top to bottom only to find out that he's married. Fuck my life! Ty thought.

He extended his hand, "Hello ma! My name is Nasir. I came over here to find out why I haven't had the pleasure of meeting you before?" he asked with a smooth demeanor.

Little do you know you're giving me all the pleasure right now, Ty thought as she squeezed her legs together to try and stop the throbbing she felt between them.

"Hi Nasir. My name is Tyquasia, but you can call me Ty."

"I hadn't got to that point yet, but are you saying I can call you?" Nasir asked with a slick smile showing off his pearly whites.

"That was cute and real slick," Ty said batting her eyelashes a little more than she needed to.

"I just wanted to make you smile; that's all. So are you here alone?" Nasir asked.

"No, I'm actually here with my friend. She went to find a waitress. She should be back any minute now," Ty said.

"Looking for a waitress? Nawh, I can't have my VIP guests on the hunt for a waitress. What did you want to order?"

Ty smiled, "I want to order a bottle of Remy and a bottle of peach Ciroc." She thought that Nasir was going to go to the bar and place her order, but instead he pulled out a walkie talkie and spoke into it, "I need a bottle of Remy and a bottle of peach Ciroc ASAP and not a minute later. There should always be a waitress in rotation in the VIP area. I need that to happen now!"

No one ever responded.

Wait a minute he works here dressed like this? Well, he's making demands so maybe he's the boss or manager, Ty thought.

"Listen ma, I got to get back to work right now, there's so much shit that ain't in order right now. Shit got to be right in less than an hour. How about you give me your number so I can hit you up sometime and put you on my permanent guest list when I'm in town?

Ty was both confused and disappointed because he already belonged to someone legally. Although skeptical, Ty took the phone from his hand and entered her name and number. By the time she finished, Khia was walking up cheesing with two waitresses totting bottles, ice and champagne flutes.

Nasir said his goodbye to Ty, and spoke to Khia before hustling his way down the stairs. Khia got up close to Ty so she wouldn't have to yell or talk loud.

"I can't leave yo' ass alone for a couple of minutes without you snagging the finest nigga in the club's attention. Do you know how long I have been coming here trying to get his attention and never got more than a brush pass when he was in the mist of running around making' sure things were right?" Khia spit with jealousy.

"We were just chatting, nothing major. He was just making sure I was ok 'cause he saw me sitting alone," Ty replied still thinking about his smile.

"Uh uh, do you know who that is girl?" Khia asked peaking Ty's interest.

"No, but I'm sure you're about to tell me," Tyquasia responded.

"You and your slick mouth…anyway, you're right I am goin' to tell you. That is Nasir Cruz, one of—if not the hottest—

club and party promoter in the South. If you want your party to be jumpin', you go to him to assure it. He's the promoter for YMCMB's party tonight. He does all the celeb parties in Miami, Atlanta, Orlando, Tampa, Texas and more." Khia said over excited.

Tyquasia couldn't believe her fuckin' luck. She'd just met and gave her number to a dude who was making legit money. He had been such a gentlemen to her. Ty decided to play it off as if she didn't care. "Oh, well. Girl, he's married; and I got a man, so it doesn't matter."

"Fuck that!" Khia said sipping on a drink one of the waitresses had just handed her. "What's sexier than a man with a lot of legit money? So what if he got a wife. That man is the definition of FINE with all capital letters and he's paid beyond belief. I bet he's getting paid well over seventy thousand dollars just for putting this party together tonight. Benzino ain't here, so what he don't know won't hurt him. Shit, plus I need to know if he got a friend for me, but that nigga got to have money too," Khia said finishing off her drink.

"I don't mean to interrupt, but is there anything else I can get for you ladies right now?" the waitress with the black and blonde ombre styled hair asked.

"No, this is good for now. How much do I owe you?" Ty asked opening her clutch.

"This bill, and anything else you order, will be taken care of. I'll be making my rounds again soon to check on ya'll. You ladies enjoy yourself."

"See what did I tell you? I bet Nasir paid for this. He likes you girl," Khia said gulping down yet another drink.

"Girl hush up talking about these men. Let's get up and… what you like to say, 'shake our asses' and enjoy our night,"

Ty replied not really meaning it because her mind was, in fact, on Nasir. She wanted to get to know more about him. He moved her insides, made her pussy throb, and she didn't even know him yet. The crazy part was she hadn't thought about Benzino once since they'd been out.

Chapter Two
Shit Just Got Real

After a long night of partying, Ty slept in. It was well after five o'clock when she woke up to the sound of her phone ringing. Head pounding, and eyes still closed, she felt around on the bed for her phone. When she didn't feel it, she followed the loud sound of her ringer and eventually found the phone lying right next to the bed on the floor. She peeked through one eye and slid the talk button to the side, "Hello," Ty said in a groggy voice.

"Yes, hello Ms. Roberts, my name is Chris and I am Benzino's lawyer. I've been trying to catch up with you since last night when I left my visit with Benzino. I came by your house, but I guess you weren't home. Right now it's not looking too good for Benzino. He's a convicted felon who was caught in possession of a firearm. I can tell you one thing I know for sure, he will do some time in prison. How much time is the only question." Chris said all in one breath.

This was too much for Tyquasia to take in; she had a hangover, and hearing what Chris just told her made her head pound even more.

"Wait a minute, I thought Benz was just arrested on a traffic stop and unpaid tickets. I didn't know it was this serious," Ty said in disbelief, suddenly regretting the fact that she'd went out last night.

A felon? I thought I knew everything about Benz. He never told me that he'd been to prison before. Tyquasia thought, her mind running rampant.

"I will be in contact with you as I get updates. I was also told to tell you to head over to Amscot and put some money on the house phone and your cell phone. I'll talk to you later," Chris said.

All Ty could say was, "Ok."

It was time for her to sober the hell up and get over the hangover that she was currently experiencing. She figured what better way to shake it off than a cold shower. She headed to the bathroom and allowed the water to wake her up. But even after she put on some clothes and threw her hair in a loose ponytail with Chinese style bangs, the thoughts of her conversation with Chris wouldn't go away.

"A fuckin' convicted felon!" she kept repeating under her breath.

When she went through the missed calls on her phone, she saw ten from an unknown name and unknown number; she knew it couldn't have been anybody else but Benzino trying to contact her. The other missed calls were from D, Khia, and Ty's mother. The last thing she saw was a text from Khia thanking her for the night out and asking her why she hadn't told her Benz was locked up.

I guess the shit is out now. I wonder if Khia knows things about Benz that I don't know. She did hang with him and his boys on the block, Ty thought.

Ty wanted answers, and who better to get them from than the man himself. The twenty-four hour Amscot is where she headed. She followed his instructions, but she was only putting money on her cell phone. Who was he to make demands from behind bars? What was the worse he could do, curse her out over the phone or through his lawyer? If he wasn't telling her the truth then she would be done—done with him for good. All this time he'd been filling her head with some getting out of the game and going legit bullshit. She knew it was all a lie.

That nigga went to prison, got out and then went right back to doing the same shit. Dumb ass dude! Ty thought shaking her head.

Once she put the money on her phone she decided to stop at Nemesis Urban Bistro to get something to eat and get her mind wrapped around everything she'd found out in the last couple of hours. She ordered a light appetizer which was Tuscan sushi. Ty finished that off followed by scallop and grilled bread sitting on top of tomato saffron sauce. As she ate, she continued to think that maybe things that were happening with Benzino were happening to open up room for her to go to school like she'd wanted to do for a long time. He was most likely getting prison time, so he wouldn't be around to stop her. The only thing that she did worry about was how she would pay for nursing school. She'd already made up her mind that she didn't want to take out any loans.

Something will come through. Maybe I should sell some of that jewelry Benz brought me and Ebay some of those clothes I've never worn that are just sitting on my side of the closet, Ty thought.

While riding in her 2012 pearl colored Dodge Nitro with the cream interior, her cell phone began to ring. She knew it had to be Benzino, so she picked up the phone without even looking at the screen.

"Hello," Ty said. Then she pressed one and his voice came through the phone blaring as he snapped.

"Yo', where the fuck have you been? I get locked up for a couple of fuckin' days and you already showing your ass! When the fuck did you start goin' to the club poppin' bottles? You already know LIV is my spot. Allure and I are always there. He saw your ass there with that lil' freak bitch Khia. I told you I didn't want you hangin' with her. You'll end up with a fucked-up reputation out there in them streets. What's gone happen if I end up doing some real time? You gone be round there with Khia in every nigga you think got money face? You supposed to be my ride or die forever chick," Benzino said finally taking a breath.

"Baby, honestly it wasn't like that. I just get so tired of being cooped up in the house, so when you told me you were locked up, instead of staying in the house stressing about it, I called Khia and we went out and had a couple of drinks; nothing major. I'm still down for you. It's us forever; all I need is the ring," Ty said telling half of the truth.

"Don't just tell me you got me, show me you got me. Keep money on ya phone and answer that muthafucka when I call. Don't try to bring yo' ass to none of my court dates, I don't want you there. You don't need to see me in these dusty ass orange jumpers. Do you think you can stay in the house for two days until we find out what my future is looking like?" Benzino asked sarcastically.

"Yeah, I can stay in the fuckin' house until then. Let me just say this, I'm getting real tired of…"

"Never mind what you're getting tired of. You're not the one sitting yo' ass in here. Our time is almost up, I'll call you later to tell you good night," Benzino said and then the phone went dead.

This muthafucka doesn't get it; you can't be the man making demands on me while you're locked up. Those workers under him are the only fuckers he can do like that; but not me, I won't stand for it!" Ty thought.

She talked a lot of shit behind Benz's back, but she did what he said and kept her ass at home. Benz had sent Chris, his best friend and business partner Allure, and a couple of trusted workers by the house to check on her a few times a day within the two days. If Ty really wanted to start some shit, she could've put a bug in Benzino's ear about how his right-hand man tried to get a little sample of paradise during one of his checkups. Allure was fine as hell, but she wasn't trying to go there with him. Her mind was elsewhere.

She'd been having the same reoccurring dream every night since Benzino had been arrested. It started off with: *Ty stepping out of the steaming hot shower, making her way into the master bedroom dripping wet. She smiled at the master piece of a man sitting on the edge of her bed. He rose up slowly, starring deep into her eyes. He picked her up and kissed her passionately as she wrapped her legs around him. Collapsing onto the bed, Ty slid down onto his hardness and began to ride him in a backwards cow girl position.*

Her complete attention was on pleasing him so every time she rose up she would contract her inner muscles. The feeling of her sliding back down drove him wild. He'd taken all he could from her ride and turned her over into a doggy-style position. His movement was non-stop. He wanted nothing more than to bang her back out. She kept up with him stroke for stroke. It was amazing, the deeper he went, the harder his nuts banged her clit; sending waves of pleasure

*through her. Her moans grew louder and louder. The fact
that he hit her G-spot at the same time he stimulated her clit
was too much. She couldn't hold it in, "Nasir! Ahh Nasir!
I'm cummmmmmmin!" Ty yelled.*

*"Fuck, I'm right behind you baby. Ummm. Ahhhhhh!"
Nasir howled, shooting a load of hot cream into her awaiting
tunnel before he lay back down on the bed.*

Tyquasia woke up yet again; sweating and soaking wet
between her legs. *That shit felt so real, so right. Damn!
Why the hell am I still dreaming about a nigga that had the
audacity to take my number and not even call me? I need to
get his ass off of my mind,* Ty thought. She pushed Nasir, and
the dream to the back of her mind so that she could focus on
getting her day started.

After a shower and cooking a tasty meal, Ty relaxed down
stairs in the home theatre. She turned the screen on to LMN.
She'd been watching movies for a few hours and was just
starting to doze off when her phone rang. She pressed one as
soon as the automated voice began to talk. She didn't have
any sweet greetings for Benz. She had questions that needed
to be answered.

"Are you a convicted felon?" Those were the first words
out of Ty's mouth.

"Ty, baby where did you hear that from?" Benzino asked.
Fuck this is not what I need right now, Benzino thought.

"Don't play with me Benzino, answer the fuckin' question."

"Yo', watch yo' fuckin' mouth when you're speakin' to
me! Looks like my not being around has got you actin' up.
To answer your question, yeah I'm a convicted felon. So the
fuck what!" Benzino yelled.

"How long were you locked up, and why hadn't you ever

mentioned that bit of very important information to me?" Ty asked.

"You don't need to know how long I was locked down, just know I did the time and it's a part of my past, so what's the use of bringing it up now?" Benz asked.

"It matters to me. I don't even know if you are who you've been telling me all this time that you are!" Ty said, this time yelling.

"Stop actin' stupid! You know me. We've been together too long for you not to know me. I didn't call you for this shit. Let me tell you what the fuck is going on. The judge trippin', talkin' 'bout he thinks it's only right that I serve out the rest of my time on the old case that I got out early on for good behavior. He sentenced me to ten years for this lil' shit. I already have Chris working on getting an appeal. I think I'm still good; so don't be worrying and shit," Benzino said. "Hello Ty…you still there? You don't have anything to worry about 'cause even in here I'll be taking care of you out there. I had some funds put away in that box at the back of the closet. You know the one I got you for your birthday. All I'm askin' is that you do this time with me as my ride or die, and you'll be taken care of while doing so."

"I'm here Benz. I just don't understand how you expect me to be there for a lying, two-time convicted felon." *What the hell is he talking about a box at the back of the closet that he got me for my birthday? He never gave me a box for my birthday.* Ty thought, but instead of saying anything, she left it alone. There had to be a reason for that lie, and as soon as they got off the phone she would go find out exactly what he was talking about.

"You love me right? You said it's us forever, so let's make

that shit happen. Will you marry me Tyquasia Roberts?" Benz asked sounding sincere.

Ty sighed, "Yes, I'll ride with you Benz. It's you and me forever; so, yes, I will marry you," Ty lied. There was no way in hell she would marry him and be tied down while he was locked up. She couldn't and wouldn't do it because she knew that if the roles were switched and the tables were turned, his ass would've forgotten about her two seconds after she announced she was going to prison for any amount of time.

"That's my girl. This line is about to hang up, but I want you to know I love you and I will call you tomorrow. Stay in tonight though. I don't want to hear about you shaking your ass in the club. I'll be spending the rest of my day working out. I just need to clear my head," Benzino said.

"I love you too Benz. Talk to you tomorrow. Keep your head up," Ty replied.

Before Benzino could reply the automated voice came on informing her that their time had ran out. Benzino probably was mad, but Ty was happy as hell. She couldn't wait to check out the "box" Benz spoke of.

She made it to their spacious closet in no time flat. When she walked in and viewed the space, it seemed quite different since she was looking at it from a different view. This time she wasn't just running in, raffling through tons of clothes, trying to find something to wear. The closet still seemed the same, but her view of it was different. She went to the back of the closet and began looking through all of her old shoe boxes, but found nothing except old, out-of-season heels that she needed to get rid of. Ty stood there and observed every detail of the closet thinking about what Benz said, *there are funds put away in that box at the back of the closet. You know the box I got you for your birthday. That had to be code for something,* Ty thought.

Ready to give up looking for the mystery box, Ty took one last glance at the space in front of her and her eyes met the picture hanging on the back of the closet's wall. She'd never really paid it much attention, but it was now starting to look like it was there for no real reason. It seemed out of place.

Who puts a picture with an Aztec design in a closet? Ty wondered.

She tried to pull the picture off of the wall, but it wouldn't budge. She ran her fingers around the frame pulling every couple of inches until her fingers hit a button. She pressed down on the button, heard a click, and the picture came away from the wall in the motion of an opening door, revealing a safe with a spin combination lock on it.

Benz must've been talking in code when he said he got this for my birthday, she thought.

For a while she just stood there staring at the combination lock trying to figure out what the code to open it could be. She tried a few different numbers and then it hit her, "My date of birth!" Ty hollered out in excitement. She twisted the numbers from left to right—020990.

Click! The safe popped open and Ty's face immediately lit up. Not only were there stacks of cash with thousand dollar bands wrapped around each stack, but there was also jewelry and DVDS marked with different dates on them; some dates as recent as being within the last couple of months.

Ty picked up one of Benzino's gym duffle bags, emptied out all of the contents and filled the bag with all of the money and jewelry from the safe. She then took a couple of the

DVDs and headed back down to the home theater. She put the first DVD in and sat back with the remote making sure that the bag was close to her. She pressed play. Benzino came on the screen, naked as the day he was born, dick slanging and all while he attempted to adjust the lens. When the lens finally came into focus, it showed that the recording was not taking place in their home.

What the fuck is this? It looks like he's at a hotel. We haven't had sex anywhere else but here since my birthday three years ago, Ty thought.

"Bring that ass over here. Don't worry about the damn camera, you know I like this kinky shit. I want you to perform for the camera," Benz said as a built woman walked into the camera's view. She was tall for a woman. She reached Benz's shoulders, so she had to be about 5'11". Her face was strong, but her makeup was flawless. She had an awful lace front on that didn't fit her at all. The outfit she wore looked nice and fit her solid frame like a glove.

Tyquasia's blood began to boil as she watched the whole scene unfold. Benz was like a different person on the camera. He wasn't soft and nurturing to the woman's every need; instead he was rough and to some degree disrespectful.

"Now you gone get down on your knees and suck dis dick! When I bust, you better swallow every drop you hear me?" Benzino asked in a demanding tone.

Without response, the woman dropped to her knees, grabbed his dick in her hand massaging it and proceeded to suck it. She sucked it as if she had been there before—like she already knew his spots. Her head glided back and forth on his dick. Something caught Ty's eyes mid bobble—the built woman's throat.

"It can't be," Ty whispered. Tears welled up in her eyes. The woman, who Ty had assumed was a well-built woman the entire time, had an Adam's apple just as big as any grown man's.

She continued to watch the video. Benz's legs started to tremble, his head fell back and he grabbed a handful of the wig the cross dresser was wearing. Benzino pulled the man's head back and came all over his face. The last drops dripped from his penis and the wig-wearing man lapped it all up with his tongue extended out of his mouth—making sure not to miss a drop.

Ty was utterly disgusted and felt sick to her stomach. Her whole body trembled. It took all she had not to throw up the contents of her stomach. She fast forwarded the video just to be sure that her eyes weren't playing tricks on her. As the video rolled, the wig-wearing man took off his mini skirt and lace boy shorts showing that his averaged-sized dick was tucked and taped to the back, giving the illusion that he had a vagina.

"Delicious, bend that ass over!" Benz demanded, taking the drag queen by the neck and putting him in the exact position he wanted him in. The man that Benz acknowledged as "Delicious" didn't fuss or fight.

"I love it when you're so demanding Daddy!" Delicious said with a raspy voice trying a little too hard not to sound like a man.

"Shut the fuck up! Didn't I tell you you're not to speak while we're on camera? When I watch this shit later, I want to catch a nut. That ain't going to happen with me hearing your voice," Benz said while picking up a condom from the night stand next to them.

At least the sick bastard used condoms, was all Ty could find good out of the situation, because ever since the first time she and Benz had sex, they never used condoms because Benz wanted her to have his baby.

She continued to watch the video as Benz picked up some KY jelly off of the night stand, rubbed it on his hard dick, and then around Delicious's ass hole. Without warning he plunged into his ass full throttle.

That's all it took to send the contents of Ty's breakfast all over her lap and on to the floor. She cried out, uncontrollably screaming, "Why me? What did I do to deserve this shit? I damn near gave up everything for this man and here he is fucking a man! Whhhy?"

She cut the DVD off and just sat there hurt, angry, confused and embarrassed. She wondered how many people knew about this. She sat there in her own pity for a while until she realized that Benz was a gay man putting on a front for the world around him.

I'm the one coming out on top. This shit here is for the birds. Why the hell am I crying? I'm the bitch with the money, car, clothes and house. I'm going to do what I should've been doing all along—take my ass to nursing school. Thank you Benzino, you and your sick antics just did me a favor, Ty thought.

She got up with the duffle bag in hand and headed to Benz's office. There were a few things she needed to look up, starting with a twenty-four hour moving company that specialized in packing and moving. Once she got that out of the way, she took a quick shower. It was time for a new life.

* * * * *

Ty headed over to her mother's new apartment, she had moved out of the projects courtesy of Benzino. Things were about to be moving at a fast pace within the next day or two, so Ty needed to tell her mother her plan now before things got hectic.

Diane was so excited to see her only living child. About seven years earlier Tyquasia's brother Tyrese had been killed in a drive-by shooting. The people who killed him were never caught. The hood speculated who it might've been, but no one knew for sure. That's why Diane tried her hardest to keep Tyquasia on the right track. She wanted better things for her daughter.

"Give me a hug Tyquasia," Diane said pulling Ty into a tight hug. "Don't you ever let six months pass without coming to see me. You know I'm not going to come to your house. I'm sorry…I just don't like that man of yours. Something about him doesn't sit too well with me. Come on in baby."

Diane and Tyquasia looked a lot alike in their facial features except Diane was a shade darker. She was forty-seven and didn't look a day over thirty. Standing at about 5'6" and weighing 150 pounds, Diane had a nice shape for a woman who'd had two kids.

"Mom stop all that. I know I gotta come by more, it's just that I've had a lot going on lately. I'm grown now; I can take care of most things on my own. I came here to talk to you about something. I don't know if it's going to make you feel better or just make you worry more."

"Don't tell me you're pregnant. Damn! I knew this shit was going to happen. I told you that this would happen. All he wants is for you to be barefoot, pregnant, and available at his command," Diane said walking away shaking her head.

Ty was not in the mood for her mother's ranting and raving so she thought it best to get right to the point of her visit.

"No, I'm not pregnant; you know I'm on birth control. I told you I have goals beyond Benzino. And stop talking about how much you don't like him especially since you have no problem with the fact that he moved you out of the projects, put you in this nice apartment, and pays the rent up for you every year. Now what I came here to tell you is that I will be leaving within the next couple of days. When I say, "leaving" I mean that I'm moving to Orlando or Atlanta. I'm ready to go to nursing school. I may need you to help me settle in. I'll know exactly where I'm moving to no later than tomorrow morning, and I've already contacted a packing and moving company so you don't have to worry about that," Ty said trying to get everything out without crying. She was still emotional over what she'd watched her man of three years doing on camera.

"Looks like you've gotten some sass in your ass since you've been away; you better watch it missy. Let's be clear here, I didn't ask him to move me anywhere. He did it to try to get on my good side. Now when you say you're moving, does that mean you and Benzino?" Diane asked sipping on what Tyquasia knew to be wine.

"Whatever ma. Benz is locked up. He doesn't know that I'm leaving, that's why I'm trying to make this happen in such a short period of time. I want to be gone before he can get wind of anything," Ty replied.

"In that case, hell yeah I'll help baby; whatever you need.

I want you to call me as soon as you find out where you'll be moving to. Shoot, I might just move too. You know I can't be that far away from you, especially with you going to a whole other city or state. We'll talk about that later though. Do you want something to eat? I'll fix your favorite," Diane said.

I really don't have the patience to deal with her moving with me. I already know she'll be over bearing; wanting to know what I'm doing, who I'm with and where I'm at. I can't deal with that, Ty thought.

"I'll make sure I call you. I'm not going to stay for dinner though. I need to get home, do some research on different schools and look up some condos and apartments. I'll call you in the morning mama. I love you," Tyquasia said bending down to give her mother a kiss on the cheek.

"Ok baby, don't forget. Be safe and I love you more," Diane said hugging Ty back tightly as if she didn't want to let her go. "You're not too grown for me to walk you to the door," Diane said walking Ty to the door and giving her another hug.

* * * * *

"Hey sexy! How's it going?" D asked.

Ty's heart warmed at the sound of D's raspy voice. "It's not going too well. I just found out a lot of shit about the man I have been with for the last, damn near, four years. I'm leaving him D. I just can't do it anymore. I've overlooked everything else, there's no way I will overlook this," Ty replied somberly.

"What the fuck is goin' on down there? Do you need me to come back, 'cause I can be on the next flight leaving out." D spazzed out at the sound of the hurt in Tyquasia's voice.

"No, I'm fine D. I can handle me. I just wanted you to know that I'm leaving Miami and moving to Atlanta to start a new life. Calm down, I will call you and keep you updated once I'm settled in there."

"Alright! You know I'll do anything for you, so if you need me, don't hesitate to call me and I'll be there."

"I know D. Trust me I do. Talk to you soon," Ty said as she hung up the phone with a smile on her face.

* * * * *

Ty knew she wouldn't be able to sleep properly until she got an official test done for HIV and every STD known to man. She wasn't going to take the risk of possibly being the carrier of something she'd contracted from Benzino. Even though she felt fine, she had to be sure, so the day before she was set to leave she went to her doctor and had him perform the necessary tests.

Her doctor informed her that the results wouldn't be back for at least two weeks. When Ty informed her doctor that she would be moving out of town, he gave her papers to sign allowing his office to call her and give her the results over the phone; which they usually didn't do. He also told her that if her results weren't good, they would ask her to come back to Miami.

She left the office with one burden lifted, but another burden weighing her down. Two weeks and that burden would be lifted as well.

Chapter Three

The Start of a New Life

Within two days, Ty successfully packed and moved her things to Atlanta, Georgia. She'd found a great two bedroom, two bath, lavish apartment home in Windsor at Midtown. She was in love with her new space. A refreshing new start was all she needed and more; with a fabulous courtyard, a majestic fountain and the breathtaking Atlanta skyline views—Ty was in awe of everything her new life had to offer.

She decided to let her mother help her with the move, but she made it very clear that Diane was only to stay a week or two while she got settled in. Once everything was unpacked and Ty had enrolled at Georgia State University, a school that offered one of the top nursing programs in the south, her mother would return back to Miami. Diane was willing to go along with Ty's wishes; all she really wanted was to spend one-on-one time with her daughter.

Ty got an early start, her first stop was at the university. After going through the enrollment process, which took up a lot of her day, Ty met up with her mother to have a light lunch and do some furniture shopping. They rode to different furniture stores, disagreeing on what styles they should go for to decorate the rooms in her apartment.

"Ma, our styles have always been very different. I've always had a more colorful, artistic and eclectic type of style; and let's face it, you have a bland, one dimensional, standard colors type of style. We just have different tastes in that regard." Ty said checking the price on a five piece cherry wood bedroom set that she'd fallen in love with from the moment they walked in the door.

"I'm hip too. I can be eclectic too; it's just that I'm more laid back with my style. All those labels and shit don't move me, as long as it looks good, I like it; no matter what name is on it. Now that cherry wood over there is nice, but that dark chocolate wood over there looks so much better on that sleigh bed," Diane said.

"You wouldn't know 'eclectic' if it slapped you in the face ma," Ty giggled. "I'm not feeling this manual, step-by-step shopping; let's just go. I'll order the things I want online and have them delivered. That's much easier. We're staying back at the hotel room again tonight, so don't go ordering all that room service like you did last night. I think we should go out to eat at a nice restaurant tonight. What do you think?" Ty asked.

"Keep on talking about my style and I'm gonna show you a lil' something. See all that y'all call 'trends' now-a-days is what I wore back in the days when I was a teeny bopper. Now back to what you were saying, I would love to go out to eat at one of those nice, high-class restaurants I'm always reading about," Diane replied with a little sass in her walk.

* * * * *

They were dressed and ready to step out by eight o' clock that night.

"Let's stop by the front desk and see where there's a nice restaurant around here for us to eat at," Ty suggested.

They stopped in the lobby and a middle aged woman at the front desk told them that Rathbun's was a great place for dinner. They got the address from her and once it was put into their GPS system, they were on their way. The restaurant was exquisite and after looking over the wide variety of items on the menu, Ty decided on Thai beef salad with a side of eggplant fries.

"What are you having ma? I know you're always eating something extra healthy, but we're out tonight; let your hair down and live a little."

"Live a little huh? Well, since you say it like that...I think I'll be having the curried chicken tenderloin with crispy tofu and I'm even going to order dessert. This gooey toffee cake with Jack Daniel's ice cream has my sweet tooth acting up," Diane smiled.

"That's what I'm talking about! All of that sounds good except that tofu," Ty frowned up. "I'll be back. I'm going to run to the bathroom. Please order for me when the waitress comes back with our drinks," Ty said excusing herself to the bathroom.

Halfway to the bathroom, Ty's phone began to ring. She continued walking to the bathroom as she dug in her purse to retrieve her phone. When she pulled it out and looked down to see who was calling, she bumped right into someone. Before the person could turn around Ty began apologizing.

"I am so sorry. I was looking at my phone and not paying any attention to where I was..." her words got caught in her throat. *What the hell is he doing here? Did he know I was here?* Ty thought.

"Heeey…Ty...quasia, right?" he asked awkwardly.

"Yep, that's me. How are you Nasir? What brings you to Atlanta?" Ty asked staring into his eyes. He looked even sexier than he did the first time they met.

"I've been good. Thanks for asking. Atlanta is actually where I call home. What brings you to Atlanta?" Nasir asked checking out Ty from head to toe in a very discreet manner; but not discreet enough to avoid his wife catching his roaming eyes.

Lorraine stood there watching her husband size another woman up as if she wasn't all the woman he needed. She couldn't take anymore. "Uh mmh," she said clearing her throat and rolling her eyes.

"Damn! Excuse my manners; let me introduce you to my wife. Tyquasia, this is Lorraine. Lorraine, this is Tyquasia."

"Nice to meet you Ty-Quesha," Lorraine spat before turning her attention to Nasir. "Baby, I don't think I want to eat here anymore. I'm ready to go," Lorraine stated.

Ty was pissed. *Did this bitch really just go there like she didn't just hear my name clearly? Let me calm down before I beat this Slim Jim looking bitch's ass and take her man at the same damn time,* Ty thought.

"My name is Tyquasia. Remember it, you might be hearing, seeing or speaking it again," Ty said with a wink. "Enjoy your evening." Ty sashayed her way to the bathroom; hips swinging from side to side with each stride. When she got inside she busted out laughing. *Got that bitch,* she thought. It was one time that she was happy Benz had called. She had to make a quick call to her girl though.

"I was just about to call yo' ass and check on you. I just know you didn't get to Atlanta and start acting brand new.

Did you see my call earlier today?" Khia popped as soon as she got on the phone.

"Pause…when you called me earlier I was picking out furniture. Now back to the reason I called you, I'm not able to talk long because I'm at dinner with my mom; you know how that goes. You wouldn't believe who I just ran into. When I say, "ran" into, I do mean it literally," Tyquasia said with lots of excitement.

"Bitch who? Tell me. You know I hate playing guessing games."

"I swear you're no fun. Anyway, it was Nasir and his high sadity ass wife. The bitch fucked up my name so I had to get her together. I used one of your moves and told her, 'My name is Tyquasia. Remember it, you might be hearing, seeing or speaking it again later.' Then I hit her with the, 'Enjoy your evening' line and I winked at both of them and kept it moving. I bet she probably still hasn't picked her mouth up off of the floor. She's going to be asking him all kinds of questions."

"Look at the shit I'm missing being stuck back here in Miami. I told you you should've taken me with you to help you get settled in, and to break the city in all at once. I would've loved to have been there for that just so I could gag in the snooty heffa's face," Khia huffed.

"I knew if you were here we would've been mopping the floor with her ass. I don't like to get my hands dirty. She definitely wasn't worth it. Look, I gotta go. I know my mom is wondering what happened to me. I'll call you later; and chill out; I told you I'll fly you up here as soon as I'm settled in. Shoot, I need somebody here to keep me sane. Bye girl," Ty ended the call and washed her hands. Her urge to use the bathroom was gone. She headed back to the table where her mother was patiently waiting on her.

"There you are. The food just arrived. Who was that lovely young couple I saw you talking to?" Diane asked.

"Oh, that was nobody. I wasn't watching where I was walking and I accidently bumped into them." Ty said with a wide grin while thinking about the topic of their conversation.

* * * * *

"Who the hell was that lil' bird Nasir? You told me once we got married I wouldn't have to deal with the disrespectful groupies anymore." Lorraine said in an eerily calm voice as she sat on the passenger side of Nasir's Rolls Royce Phantom.

She had a piercing stare that interrupted his sexual thoughts of Tyquasia. He was there in physical form, but mentally, Nasir was somewhere under a rainfall making passionate love to Ty. He knew after the little stunt Ty pulled with the name droppin' towards his wife, that he would be in for a long, drawn out night of questions and nagging.

"You know you're sexy when you're mad, don't you? All that wasn't even called for sweetie. You messed up that woman's name on purpose; you and I both know that. I've known you for five years, been married to you for three; I know you. I don't really know her, we met when I was down in Miami promoting and putting together the YMCMB party. She loved how the party turned out and asked me to do a party for her birthday. I thought her number was stored in my phone, but when I looked for it to give to Joy so that she could get a meeting set up, it wasn't there," Nasir said halfway telling the truth. He glanced at Lorraine to see if she was buying his story. Her facial expression hadn't changed, so he turned his attention back to the road.

Lorraine looked out of the window with a slight smile. She knew all about the number because she was the one who deleted it. Every time Nasir came home from those "business trips" she couldn't stand, she would check his phone and delete any new female's name and number. She knew he wasn't that slow, he had to know something was going on 'cause he now had put a lock pattern to get into his phone.

"I wasn't paying y'all any attention when her name was mentioned. Your story of how y'all met sounds kind of fishy, but I don't even want to talk about it. Let's just go home so I can eat and prepare for my flight in the morning," Lorraine said.

G STREET CHRONICLES
A NEW URBAN DYNASTY
WWW.GSTREETCHRONICLES.COM

Chapter Four

On The Right Track!
Two Weeks Later...

"Hello, can I speak to Tyquasia Roberts?" A woman with a sweet voice asked.

"Speaking." Ty replied already knowing what the call was about.

"Ok Ms. Roberts, my name is Rhonda. Can you give me your date of birth and the last four digits of your social security number please? I want to confirm that this is in fact Tyquasia Roberts."

If it wasn't for the woman's sweet voice, Ty probably would've cursed her out. She had been on pins and needles for two weeks waiting on the results from her tests. No one else knew about her getting tested, so she couldn't share her nervousness with anyone.

"My date of birth is February 9, 1990 and the last four digits of my social are 1207," Ty said annoyed.

"Well, Ms. Roberts, I have great news; your test results came back all clear. You are HIV negative and STD free. My advice for you as such a young woman, is to be careful out here, most of these men don't mean you any good."

"You don't know how happy I am. You just made my day Rhonda. Thank you for calling, and you're right; these men don't mean any good, even when they act like they do."

"Keep that in mind always. I see that you will no longer be a patient at this office, so I have taken it upon myself to print out a list of excellent doctors in your new area. I will be mailing the list out to you today. I like to look out for young people as much as I can. Keep your health up. Let me get off of this phone running my mouth, I have so much work to do. There were some people who weren't so lucky in the results they got, so be thankful. Have a good day."

"Trust me Rhonda, I am very thankful. I'll take heed to the advice you have given me. You do the same and try to have a good day as well. Goodbye."

What a nice woman. I'm so happy I can finally breathe freely without a worry. If that bastard had of given me anything, they would've been putting me in his cell after putting him six feet deep in the ground. Thank you Lord.

* * * * *

"Hurry up, shut the door. My mother didn't see you, did she?" Ty asked.

"No, she didn't see me. When you texted me and said y'all were pulling up I went into the little café so that I could see her when she walked pass. She didn't look too happy by the way. Miss Diane needs to chill out sometimes," Khia replied as they pulled off.

"Girl, she didn't want to go home even after I got settled into my apartment. The only reason she's finally leaving now is 'cause yesterday I called my Aunt Pam and begged her to ask my mother to go back to Miami to celebrate her birthday with her. She was driving me nuts. Anyway, I'm so glad you're here; let me fill you in with what's been going on. Dealing with my mother, school, Benzino calling all the time, and trying to enjoy and live my life, I've been going crazy."

"Well, I'm happy to be here. You're not going to have to worry about all of that stuff, we're going to have some fun; at least I plan to. I'm ready to party, meet some new ATL dick, and just enjoy my time here. Oh yeah, what's the chick's name you told me you want me to meet…the one you met at school?" Khia asked poppin' her gum.

"Her name is Paige. I can't wait for y'all to meet. She's the coolest, smartest, urban white girl you could ever meet. She reminds me of us both. She has a little bit of me and you in her," Ty replied.

"Hooray, I can't wait to meet this Paige character," Khia said sarcastically.

"Don't be like that. She's cool people and she's going to be around a lot while you're here. We have almost every class together, so suck it up and change your attitude. Paige suggested something after hearing me talk about you, and I think it's a great idea. She suggested that you should try to get enrolled into GSU or a trade school with a nursing program here. That way we can all do our thing in getting our 'learn' on together." Ty said smiling at the thought of them all achieving something greater together.

Khia looked at Tyquasia from the corner of her eye and wanted to slap the smile off her face. "Have you forgotten that I dropped out in the twelfth grade? I didn't get my diploma. Besides, that whole school thing just ain't for me. I'm out here tryin' to get this paper anyway I can; school can wait," Khia retorted.

"I thought you were enrolled in GED classes," Ty responded.

"I never went to that shit. I don't want to talk about that, so let's just change the subject. I'm hungry, what are you cooking for dinner?" Khia asked.

"Well, I have lots of work to get done, but I think I can whip something quick up. After we drop your bags off at the apartment, and I give you get a little tour, we can go to the grocery store and get whatever we need," Ty stated.

"Sounds good to me."

* * * * *

"Khia, can you get the door? I'll be down in a minute, I'm getting dressed," Ty yelled.

Khia huffed and got up from her comfortable spot on the couch. When she opened the door and saw Paige she tried to hide her shocked expression. Paige was beautiful. She definitely wasn't like any other white girl Khia had seen before. Her style was on another level. You would think she had some African American somewhere down her bloodline 'cause her body was sick. The girl had curves galore and full, pouty lips glossed to perfection.

Who the hell does this bitch think she is? Khia thought, hatin' on Paige.

"Dang girl, are you gonna let me in? I'm not getting any younger standing out here," Paige said.

"My bad. That bag of yours is fierce," Khia said rolling her eyes as she stepped to the side.

"I'm assuming you're Khia," Paige said taking a seat where Khia had just been sitting. "It's nice to meet you. This right here is an old Michael Kors bag, you can borrow it anytime," Paige stated.

"Yep, I'm Khia. It's a cute bag, but I don't want to borrow

it. If I wanted it, I would have one of my many men go out and get it for me," Khia lied. She knew deep down that she didn't have one man that would go out and drop that type of bread on a bag for her.

"Well damn bitch! I don't know what your problem is, but jealousy…" Paige started to snap, but was interrupted by Ty walking into the room.

"Hey Paige, I'm glad y'all finally got to meet. We're about to have some fun together at the club. Y'all ready?" Ty asked oblivious to the tension in the room. She knew that once they got to know each other, the room would be full with gossip and laughter between them.

"Thank you hun. I'm ready to get some alcohol up in me. This week has been too draining. You know how we do, remember how it was the first time we went out—lots of gags and too much excitement," Paige replied.

"Ok, let's get going then. Woo, they're not going to know what to do with us when we step off in that joint," Ty said happily.

"What club did you say we were going to?" Khia asked not really feeling the idea of partying with *little miss all that*.

"We're going to the Velvet Room; one of my boy toys got us the hook up there," Paige replied as she applied a touch of gloss to her lips.

Khia didn't say anything else; she just headed out of the apartment to Ty's car.

"Oh yeah Khia, we're not going in my car. See that all white Range Rover parked over there, that's Paige's ride." Tyquasia said pointing to a nice ass white-on-white Range Rover that stood out amongst all of the expensive rides in the parking lot.

* * * * *

The club was definitely jumpin'. The who's who of Atlanta were all in attendance. They had no problem getting into VIP once Paige mentioned her man's name. They wasted no time getting their bottles of Rośe, Ciroc and Grey Goose. After a couple of drinks, Khia announced she was tired of being cooped up in the VIP area watching everybody on the dance floor having a good time. She suggested that they hit the dance floor for a little while.

"Shit, that's all you had to say. Come on let's go," Ty said.

"Paige, are you coming down to the dance floor with us?" Ty asked.

"I guess I will. Tremayne has been textin' me since we got here trying to get me on the dance floor," Paige replied.

Who the hell is that fine ass nigga staring at me? Oh shit, he's coming my way. If he's talkin' the way I like, we'll be getting a room tonight; 'cause my goodies are yearning to be eaten and I don't plan on being quiet while he's eating them, Khia thought as she imagined the sexy man dippin' between her thighs.

She turned her head so that he wouldn't see her checking him out. She then gyrated her ass cheeks making her dress rise little by little.

"Hey there handsome, I see you found me," Paige said giving Tremayne a peck on the lips and a hug.

"You know I would've looked all over for yo' ass if I had to," he said squeezing her ass. "I knew y'all had made it in 'cause my boy at the front door told me you were here when I came in."

"Let me introduce you to my girl and her friend. Tremayne

this is Tyquasia and her friend Khia."

"Nice to meet you Tremayne," Ty said looking him over, giving Paige a wink of approval.

Khia couldn't even utter any words. *Not only does this bitch have the looks, style and shape, she also has the fine ass brothers. Oh, hell no! I'm thinking this muthafucka was lookin' at me, and come to find out he was looking pass me at this bitch standing behind me. Fuck this shit! My hello kitty wants to get petted tonight and one of these niggas up in here is gonna be doing the petting,* Khia thought.

"Don't mind her Tremayne, she's rude as fuck," Paige said rolling her eyes at Khia. "Let's dance." She backed her ample ass up on him and whined to the beat of the music.

"Damn, what the hell is your problem?" Ty asked when she caught the drift of the major shade Khia had just thrown.

"Ain't shit my problem, I'm about to go find me a dancing partner. As a matter of fact, I think I see one right now," Khia said.

"Yeah, you go do that 'cause yo' ass is trippin'!" Ty yelled behind her as she walked off in the direction of a group of men.

"Sorry about that girl. I don't know what's gotten into her. I'm going to let y'all get y'all dance on while I find my way back up to the VIP area to refill my drink," Ty said.

"Yeah, something's up with her, but oh well. If I'm not here when you come back down just text me," Paige said.

"Ok, will do."

Ty walked off. She didn't know what had Khia acting out of character. She was being more moody than usual. But whatever it was, Ty wasn't going to let it ruin her night. She had a couple of tests coming up within the next two weeks, so the night out would be her last night out for a while and she planned to enjoy it.

The club was wall to wall with people and Ty practically had to squeeze through the crowd to get to where she was going

"Excuse me! Excuse me! Excuse me! Damn," Ty said. *I swear these muthafuckas act like they don't see me trying to get through. Maybe if I walked through with an attitude they would move the fuck out of my way!* Ty thought.

"No, excuse me sexy. Do you need a personal escort to your destination?" A familiar voice whispered in her ear.

A slight smile crept across her face. "If I keep running into you everywhere I go I'm going to assume you're stalking me," Ty said with a chuckle. "I will definitely take you up on that escort suggestion. I'm headed up to the VIP area."

"We both know that wouldn't be true, me stalking you... nawh since this is my city and this is another party promoted by me," Nasir said taking Ty by the hand navigating her through the crowd.

She loved the way he took control of the situation and how he guided her through the crowd. It was like everybody in the club knew who he was because when he walked through he never had to say excuse me; his presence said it for him and moved people.

It had been a little while since Ty had been able to get her treasure chest wet by a man. She'd become accustomed to handling her own business. She was never a sex toy type of chick, but when she and Paige were having a little girl talk, Paige had put Ty up on game. Paige told her that when she didn't want to be bothered with any of her boy toys, she would handle her horniness all on her own. That was all cool and dandy for a little while, but now Tyquasia wanted a manly man to scratch her itch. That manly man could possibly be Nasir.

When they reached the VIP area, Tyquasia put her plan into motion. "Nasir, I want you to tell me a little about yourself. I mean, I've seen you so much lately that I'm starting to think I know you."

"It's funny that you say that 'cause I'm feeling like I already know you too. I'll tell you a little about me, but I want to know more about you as well," Nasir said.

"Umm ok, that's fine," Ty replied.

"My name is Nasir Cruz. I was born in Atlanta, Georgia. I'm twenty-six years old and you met my wife of three years. I've owned, and have been running my own company called, Make It Happen Entertainment for the past five years," Nasir said.

Tyquasia busted out laughing.

Nasir sat there trying to figure out what he'd said that was so funny.

"I'm sorry, don't look like that. I know you're wondering why I'm laughing. It's just that where I'm from dudes don't just give you their government name with a full run down on their life. Their always too scared that you're working with the feds," Ty said continually laughing.

"Ma, I'm not worried about any of that. I make my money the legal way. I stopped slanging drugs back when I was seventeen and was given a second chance at life. The police nor the FBI can fuck with me; I'm clean." Nasir replied.

"I feel you...at least you're honest," Ty said and then looked away focusing her attention on the dance floor. For some reason, she was nervous. She knew Nasir was a married man, but she also knew she wanted a piece of him too.

"What's going on in your head?" Nasir asked placing his hand on her chin. He turned her head to face him.

"Never mind what I'm thinking about. There's nothing I can do about it anyway," Ty said.

Nasir knew where she was going with that statement. He wanted to make something happen, but he didn't know if she was ready to be involved with him on that level. "How about this, first I want you to tell me about yourself and what brings you to Atlanta. We'll discuss what's on your mind later," Nasir said genuinely interested in getting to know more about Tyquasia.

Ty told him a little about herself but not really giving the full reason why she left Miami and moved to Atlanta. Nasir was taken aback by Tyquasia. She was different than any other girl he had met before. She wasn't just a regular girl from the hood blaming her surroundings for what she did and didn't have. She wasn't the typical lazy, ignorant, *get with a baller to be on top for a second* type of chick. She was an intelligent, goal oriented, sexy woman with a bright future ahead of her. Ty wasn't infatuated with his diamonds, his status in the entertainment business, or how much money he had or what kind of car he drove. None of that seemed to matter to her. He realized quickly that Ty was just interested in getting to know him for who he was. That made his attraction for her stronger. If he could have it his way, he would sit there and talk to her all night. It seemed as though hours and a lifetime had passed by how they'd talked so much.

"I've got to go check and make sure things are running smoothly. But I want to keep in contact with you, and this time I'm going to give you my number. Hit me up tomorrow morning and we'll make plans, ok sexy?" Nasir flirted with a warm smile.

"Ok, I will do that. It was nice talking to you all this time without any interruptions," Ty replied feeling hot all over. She knew the butterflies she was feeling had everything to do with the man standing before her.

"I enjoyed talking with you as well," Nasir said as he handed her his card, kissed her gently on her forehead and whispered in her ear, "Dream about me tonight." Then he turned and walked away leaving her standing there in full bliss.

Ty knew she was all in and completely wide open for a man who was legally attached to another woman. Even with that technicality in mind, she was satisfied with how her night had turned out. She couldn't wait to get home and do just as Nasir had suggested and dream about him; especially seeing as though it wouldn't be the first time she had done so.

* * * * *

Ty floated back downstairs to round up the girls. She found Paige standing in the same spot she had left her in; chatting it up with a Dwight Howard look alike who was only missing the height.

"Hey girl, have you seen Khia?" Ty asked.

"Oh, what's up Ty? I haven't seen that chick since she walked off with that funky ass attitude of hers earlier and I haven't seen you in a while either missy," Paige replied with an observing look.

"I'll tell you about where I've been later," Ty smiled. "The club is about to let out in about ten minutes; are you ready to head out before everybody starts heading for the exits?" Ty asked.

"Yeah, let's head on out. We can wait for Khia outside, but if we don't see her she'll be on her own," Paige stated.

"Eric you have my number, call me and we'll chill sometime next week," Paige said and then slid through the crowd right behind Ty.

They walked outside and there was Khia pacing up and down the sidewalk barefoot, heels in hand, with glazed over eyes. She looked pissed and drunk as hell.

Ty walked up to make sure she was ok. "You don't look too hot, are you feeling ok?" she asked.

"Yeah, I been reeaady to go…shiiiit," Khia snapped slurring every other word.

Tyquasia took a deep breath. She wasn't about to let Khia's drunk ass ruin her night. "You can chill with the fucked up attitude. If you can't handle your liquor, you don't need to fuckin' drink. I don't know who pissed in your drink, but that sideways talkin' needs to cease," Ty snapped back. "Now bring yo' drunk ass on!"

"I can't see how you put up with her shit. A bitch was having a good night and here she goes being the sour puss of the group," Paige said as they headed to the car.

"Not you too Paige. Just don't say anything about it cause I don't want to hear her mouth," Ty said shaking her head.

"Bitccchhh, I don't know who youus talkin' bout, but you better check yo' self before I dooo," Khia slurred throwing her heels down and jumping into a fighting stance.

"You ain't even worth it boo. Look at you. Who takes their shoes off at the club and actually walks down the street barefoot? I don't give a damn how drunk I am, or how bad my feet are hurting, you won't catch me barefoot 'cause guess what? I have at least that much class!" Paige yelled.

"Bittcch, I'll knocka yous the fucck out," Khia said running towards Paige.

Good thing Ty was standing next to Khia. She caught Khia's hand mid-air, snatching the stiletto heel she was about to smash into Paige's head, out of her hand.

Paige swung a counter blow that made Khia stagger back a little. "Now bitch, you gone think twice about running up on me. I wish you would. That will be the day I play Tic Tac Toe with your fuckin' head," Paige yelled with a look on her face that said she wasn't bull shitting.

"I'm not tryna ruin your night, but that bitch..." Paige said pointing behind Ty, "ain't getting in my fuckin' truck! She has Tom and Jerry, her ass better get to footing it back to your place!"

"Paige don't do that. It's not that serious. Look at her, she's drunk as hell. She probably won't remember any of this tomorrow," Ty said trying to pull some sympathy out of Paige, but it didn't seem like it was working from the, "I don't give a fuck look" on Paige's face.

"The bitch should know how to handle her liquor," Paige said chirping the alarm on her truck. "You can hop in, but she ain't riding anywhere in my shit."

"You know I'm not going to leave her out here. She's not from here and doesn't know her way around Atlanta," Ty said feeling a migraine coming on. Standing there going back and forth with Paige was starting to aggravate her.

"I have an early morning class tomorrow so call her a cab 'cause I really need to get going," Paige said staying stern in her decision.

Tyquasia was not about to sit there and beg Paige, so she

reluctantly told her to go ahead and leave them both there. "We'll talk tomorrow," Ty said as she pulled her cell phone out of her purse.

"I could really slap your ass right now," Ty snapped looking at Khia.

"Fuck that ol' uppity bitccch…thinking she better than us. Tryna take all the niggas from us. Why she can't get some oof her own kindddd? I donnn't like her ass anyway, and I don't see why yous hanging out with her in the first place," Khia said slurring and swaying back and forth. "I should bust her fuckin' windows out while she riding pass like shit sweet."

"You're going too fuckin' far Khia. That girl ain't never did shit to you. You're still hot about that white girl who stole your boyfriend back in the eighth grade. She's not her. She can like whoever the fuck she wants to like; it's a free fuckin' country. Maybe I should've left yo' ass and rode with her. Don't say shit else until you get your mind right," Ty yelled, losing her temper and patience.

"Dooo what you gottta do thennn," Khia said trying to walk away.

Ty couldn't let her walk around drunk, so she grabbed her arm. "Come on…we're finding a way back to my place. I don't even have the number to a cab company!"

When they made it back to the front of the club, the crowd that was letting out began dispersing quickly. Ty walked up to a security guard who was standing outside and asked him if he knew the number for a cab. He told her no, but he believed his friend might know one. He then let her know that his friend would be coming out soon. She thanked him and told him when his friend came out to send him over to the bench on the other side of the street at the corner.

* * * * *

Nasir was wrapping up his business transaction with the owner of the club. He made sure to get his final payment before he left any event. The owner let him know that another one of his parties was a success and that they would be working together again real soon.

He walked out of the club dapping all of the security guards along the way; some he knew personally, others he knew from just throwing events at different clubs.

"Yo' bruh, do you still have that cab number you gave me a few months back? There's a chick and her friend that needs it if you do. They're sitting on a bench not far from the club," the security guard stated.

"These females nowadays get to the club anyway they can huh? I might have the number stored in my phone. I'll give it to them if I do. Check ya later bruh," Nasir said walking off.

Instead of walking directly over to the bench, he went and got his car so that once he gave the chicks the number he could be out. When he pulled up in front of the bench he saw one girl laying down with no shoes on; she was knocked out. When he looked at the other girl who had her back facing the road, he knew who it was immediately.

"Tyquasia, what are you doing out here?"

Ty jumped at the sound of him calling her name. She didn't want him to see her stranded at the club and sitting at a bus stop, so she decided to just start explaining.

"Hey Nasir," she said uneasily. "Umm, it's kind of a long story. I didn't drive to the club tonight. We rode with a friend of mine, and my friend Khia here…" she said pointing at the female laying on the bench. "…got into a little argument with my friend Paige. The two of them don't really like each other and Paige didn't want her riding back to my place in her car and I couldn't just leave Khia out here in the state she's in, so I stayed here with her," Ty explained.

Nasir sighed and then smiled. *Damn, she's a good friend not to leave ol' girl alone,* Nasir thought about Ty's actions.

"Go ahead and get in the car; I'll drive ya home."

Though thankful for his nice gesture, Ty didn't want to take him up on his offer.

"I can't have you do that. I'm sure your *wife* is at home waiting on you. I don't want to get you in trouble." Even though the words came out of her mouth, she didn't really mean them. She wanted him to take her home and do some things to her once they got there.

"First things first, I'm a grown ass man; therefore, I don't get in trouble. Second, my *wife* isn't a problem, but if it makes you feel any better she's not home. She's away on a business trip out of town and won't be back for a couple of days. Now get in the car," he said opening the passenger and back door. "I'll put your friend in the car."

The ride back to Ty's house wasn't a long one, but it wasn't filled with much conversation; only a light rhythm of jazz played from the radio.

So he's not blasting some loud rap music and stunting for me. I like that—a grown and sexy man on his suave shit, Ty thought.

"When you said the name of your apartments I knew they sounded a little too familiar. It's funny, I lived here for about a year when I first brought my house in Buckhead and was having it renovated and completely decorated."

Ty smiled, "Yep, this is my place for now. Pull up to that

apartment on your far left."

They got out of the car and Ty went to unlock the door while Nasir picked Khia up out of the back seat. He carried her inside. "Where is she sleeping?"

"The guest room is upstairs, but you don't have to take her up there; put her ass down, wake her up, and make her ass walk up those stairs herself," Ty said watching how Nasir carried Khia with little, to no, strain. Khia wasn't a big girl, but she had a little weight on her. She was short and solid.

"I don't want to do her like that, and if you were drunk and passed out, I wouldn't want anyone to do you like that either. Now, is it the room at the beginning of the hall or at the end?" He asked, readjusting Khia in his arms so that his climb to the top of the stairs would be much easier.

Ty sighed, "If you insist. I guess you're right; it's the first room."

Nasir winked at her and gave her a sexy smile that sent chills up the back of her neck.

Mmm...mmm...mmm! Boy, what I would do to that man, Ty thought heading towards the kitchen. She decided to put on a pot of coffee.

"She's all tucked away," Tyquasia heard him say as he made his way back downstairs.

"That's good to hear. She'll wake up in the morning and realize how she fucked my night up. I can't thank you enough for doing what you've done. There's not many men out there that would've done that without expecting something in return. Most of them would've just given me the cab number and then hauled ass." The coffee machine went off. "Oh, I almost forgot...would you like some?"

"Yeah, I would like some coffee. As you can tell, I'm

not like most men. Your night doesn't have to be all bad on account of your friend. Let's sit and keep our talk from earlier going or just watch a movie if you're not up for talking," Nasir said with a hint of lust in his voice.

"I think we can definitely make that happen. How about we do both? The DVDs are all in the entertainment center cabinets over there in alphabetical order. I'll get some snacks."

"You got some classics up in here: *Scarface*, all of *The God Father* series, *Set It Off* and *Boyz n the Hood*. I don't know what to choose from in this massive collection. I thought my brother had a lot of DVDs in his collection, but you're beating him by a long shot," Nasir said amazed.

"I take pride in my DVDs. You can pop in *Set It Off,* that's my joint right there." Ty said walking into the living room holding a tray filled with everything from popcorn to Little Debbie Cakes and two cups of coffee.

"*Set It Off* it is then. You brought all of these snacks and it's just the two of us?"

"Yeah, I didn't know what you liked," Ty replied.

They sat down on the comfortable couch with a respectable amount of room in between them. Ty, not being able to sit still, had to get up and move around a bit—busying herself with things she didn't need to be doing at the moment.

Nasir watched her move about making sure everything was right—opening snacks, turning the lights down more, and pulling the drapes closed. She looked over at Nasir who was staring back at her. Her heart raced looking at him. She suddenly felt a heat wave brush over her.

"Umm, is it a little warm in here?" she said fanning herself with her hand. She walked over to the thermostat to turn it down more even though it was already at seventy degrees.

"Nawh, I think that's all you. Come here. I feel like you're trying to avoid sitting on this couch with me." Nasir said with his eyebrow raised as if he was trying to figure out if that's what the case was.

Ty's legs moved on Nasir's command. She walked right up to him and stood there looking down at him. He pulled her down next to him. "We've been close to each other before, what's wrong with you now? Are you uncomfortable?"

"No, I'm not uncomfortable. It's just that before when we sat close to each other, it was in a crowded place. I knew nothing could happen there, but I'm not so sure right now. I don't know if I can control myself with us being alone," Ty said with a twinkle in her eyes.

"I understand; but right now I'm not looking to do anything except spend some time vibin' with you. It's not often I get to relax with a woman that I feel a connection to. I won't do anything you don't want me to do; ok?"

"Ok," Ty said relaxing a bit. She let the tension ease from her body. Other than the boys back in high school that she flirted with, had a crush on, and Benzino, Nasir was the first man to make her feel all giddy inside.

He picked the throw cover up and laid it over them. Then he picked up the tray with the snacks on it and told her to have at it. "Don't be scared to snack or eat in front of me 'cause I'm a food lover."

"Oh, trust me...I'm not scared to get my grub on."

They got a little closer and snuggled up to enjoy the movie.

* * * * *

The deep voice of Barry White started playing, stirring the sleeping couple out of their blissful sleep. The song, *My First, My Last, My Everything* stopped playing and the phone beeped, alerting that there was a new message of some kind.

Nasir squinted and grunted, not wanting to move from his comfortable position under Tyquasia. But when his phone began to ring again, he slid from under her as carefully as he could, trying not to disturb her. Little did he know Ty was already awake, but she decided to keep her eyes closed to see how things would play out. When she heard the lyrics of the song playing she knew it could only be one person; *his wife.*

Khia walked out of the kitchen chewing on a ripe banana, shaking her head. "I think you better answer that, it's been ringing for the last hour or so. Must be important."

Nasir looked at Ty to make sure she was still sound asleep; then he put his finger to his lips to hush Khia as he answered the phone trying to sound groggy.

"Uh, hello," he said.

"Baby please explain something to me, why did I come home early from a seven day business trip only to find a house with just Linda in it? I sent her on her way so that I could spend a little alone time with my husband, but I get upstairs to our bedroom and find a neatly made bed. Stop me if I'm wrong, but that means *my husband* didn't come home last night!" Lorraine practically yelled the last part. "Then I call you over fifty-five times and you don't answer. What the fuck is going on?"

"I uh…went to the after party last night at a little after-hour's spot about an hour away from the house. I was too tired to drive home so I got a room. Chill the fuck out with the way yo' ass is speaking to me like you ain't got no respect for a nigga. I thought you weren't going to be home for a couple more days anyway. Didn't you tell me Brandie booked you to speak at another school? What time is it anyway?"

"Nasir, you mean to tell me you went to an after hour party? I can't remember the last time you went to one of those whore-filled parties. You didn't have to network 'cause your name is already out there. As much as you hate staying at hotels, no matter how fancy they are, you expect me to believe you stayed at one last night? I can't believe it! Not that you really care, but I had Nancy change my appearance date so that I could come home and spend some time with you before it's time for New York's Fashion Week. You know when that rolls around, I'm going to be too busy to see you, let alone talk to you. I'm booked for three different shows, appearances and interviews all that week. I'll be leaving back out in a couple of days, so let me spend some time with you now."

"Yes, I went to the party to network; with you being somewhat in the entertainment business yourself, you should know there's no such thing as too much networking. I had a few drinks with some club owners who were in town talking future business opportunities. I got tired and got a room; it's not a fuckin' biggie. I don't understand why you're questioning me, you know how this business goes. I was doing this shit before I met you. Now I'll be home in a couple of hours," he fumed. *Click!* He hung up the phone without a second thought about it.

If there was one thing that made his blood boil more than anything, it was being questioned by a woman. So he did what he knew would make her equally as mad and simply hung up the phone and cut it off. He figured if someone needed to contact him and it was dangerously important or a matter of life or death, that person had better call 911. He rubbed his hand down his face and let out a long sigh. "Women, can't live with them, can't live without them," Nasir stated shaking his head.

Khia stood there watching him intensely. *Boy is he a sight to see, pure pleasure to my eyes. Mmm! The way he handled his wife hounding him was a straight up turn on. Damn!* Khia thought. When she got ready to say something else to him, he stopped her before she could move her lips; leaving her words stuck in her throat.

"I don't wanna hear it so save yo' smart comments. Where's the bathroom?"

"Rude much?" Khia huffed showing on the outside that she was unpleased with the way he handled her, but on the inside she beamed with excitement. *Ohhh, yesss Daddy! Shut me the fuck up again,* she thought. "The bathroom is down that hallway on your left."

"Thanks," he said as he kissed Ty lightly on the lips and headed off towards the bathroom.

When Nasir was close to the bathroom Ty popped her eyes open.

"Bitch, I know yo' ass too well. I knew you were listening to everything. One time I thought I saw you peek your eyes open and look at me real quick. So how did Mr. Promoter get here and what did you two lil' nasties do last night on the couch?" Khia asked being her nosey self.

"You know I'm not that heavy of a sleeper anyway. I'll tell you about how he got here and why you led up to the reason for him being here. We didn't do anything, but you know I wanted too. We talked, watched my favorite movie, shared a brief passionate kiss and that's about it. Girl, the man can kiss real good. I think we fell asleep watching *Set It Off* though," Ty said thinking back on last night's events.

"Hold up, I had something to do with him ending up here?" Khia asked with a confused expression.

Nasir came walking from the bathroom drying his freshly washed hands on a paper towel. "I see my sleeping beauty has awakened."

Ty played along stretching as if she'd just opened her eyes. "Yep, I'm up," she replied with a bright smile.

He slipped on his Prada shoes. "I hope you enjoyed your time last night 'cause I did and I want to spend more time with you."

"Yes, I did enjoy my time with you and I'm sure we can make that happen again; only next time we'll do it without the help of others," Ty chuckled looking in Khia's direction.

"We're going to talk later heffer," Khia said still oblivious to what went on.

"That's just what I wanted to hear. Well, I'm not too happy about this, but I have to get going. For some reason, my wife felt it was necessary to come home early from her business trip. I'll get up with you sometime today though, so don't worry about that," he said winking at Ty.

"Khia, nice meeting you even under the circumstances. If it hadn't been for you, I wouldn't even be here right now," Nasir said.

Khia paused for a second while trying to remember what went on, when she couldn't remember what happened she played along as if she knew and replied, "Yeah, no problem.

Anytime." She made a note in her head to find out what he was talking about later on from Ty.

Nasir shook his head and Ty chuckled awkwardly. "Let me get my slippers so I can walk you out to your car."

They stood by Nasir's car in a tight embrace. When he was about to release her, she raised up on her tippy toes and kissed him with as much passion as she could muster. She didn't even know she had it in her. She'd forgotten that she hadn't brushed her teeth and was probably rockin' a mouth full of morning liquor breath, but at that point it didn't matter; Nasir was enjoying it. The kiss was deep and sensual; it could've gone on forever. They were still in the moment even after their lips separated.

"What are you trying to do to me?"

Tyquasia smiled and replied using some of the same words he'd used on her last night, "I'm not trying to do anything to you that you don't want me to."

Nasir shook his head, *what am I getting myself into.* "I like that. If that's the case, then we'll be doing a lot of that real soon," he said as he gave her a quick kiss before hopping in his ride. "Have a good day sexy and we'll talk later today; ok?"

"Ok."

Ty watched him pull off. It was official, she would find a way to get around the fact that he had a wife and make him her man. She didn't like to share too much of anything, especially a man, so those arrangements couldn't last long.

Chapter Five

Tryna Keep Us Together

Lorraine sat with the phone in her hand. She was fuming. *He knows I hate it when he does that shit. Ugh!*

She called her older sister Eva. "Hey lil' sis," Eva answered joyfully.

"Hey Eva," Lorraine replied sulking.

"Uh uh! You don't sound like a woman that just shot with one of the biggest fashion companies in the world. What's wrong Raine?" Eva asked concerned, knowing from the sound of her sister's voice that something wasn't right.

"We'll talk tomorrow. Can you meet me for brunch at our spot?"

"Sure I can. You haven't seen your nephew in a while, he's getting so fat. It doesn't even seem like he's nine-months old already. I'll bring him with me."

Lorriane's spirits lifted a little at the mention of her nephew. Lord knows she had wanted a baby with Nasir for quite a while, but their jobs just wouldn't allow it. "That'll be great. See you then. Love you sis."

"I love you too. Cheer up hun."

An hour later Nasir came strolling through the door. He passed Lorraine sitting on the couch in the living room and headed for the stairs to take a shower.

"Damn, you don't see me in here? I can't get a *hey baby,* a kiss, a hug or something? I was gone for a whole fuckin' week." Lorraine was full of much attitude.

"I'm not up for your shit right now Lorraine. I just wanna take a shower and get something to eat in my stomach. Damn!" He yelled as he continued walking to the master bedroom; once he entered, he slammed the door behind him.

Mmm mmm…something definitely isn't right. He's never talked this disrespectfully to me before. Is it something I've done? Maybe I've been gone too much. Yeah, that could be what it is, Lorraine thought as she started rethinking what her schedule had been for the past couple of months.

I'm going to make it up to him; at least while I'm in town 'cause there's no way I'm missing New York Fashion Week, she thought getting up to head to the kitchen and cook. She didn't want Nasir to have a reason to leave the house, even though she was beat and just wanted to relax with a fine glass of wine.

Moments later, Lorraine was sure she had the whole house smelling up something good. She finished making one of Nasir's favorite dishes: crab shala and homemade garlic bread. He walked in the kitchen smiling. He wrapped his arms around her waist from behind. "Damn baby, you did all this for me after the way I talked to you?"

She spun around into his embrace to face him, staring deep into his eyes looking for any form of deception. Her search came up empty since he tried to focus on everything, except her deep stare.

"Yes, I did all of this for you. I know I can be a lot to handle some times and I tend to overreact on some things,

I'm working on that so bear with me. I just want you to know that I appreciate you sticking through it with me every step of the way."

It's been the same shit our whole marriage and she's been saying the same thing all along. Maybe I should've started spending the night out months ago seeing as this unhappiness has been around for a while now, Nasir thought.

"I appreciate you for being the only woman you know how to be. Remember what you told me on our wedding day, we're in this for the long run now," he kissed her on her forehead. "Come on now, let's eat."

"I'm glad you remembered that, 'cause the only way out of this here..." she pointed between them with a sharp point knife, "is a body bag." She ended with a wink and a wicked look.

Nasir looked at her and shook his head laughing, "Woman, you're so damn crazy." When he turned his back to her the look on his face told it all. He wondered if she was really crazy enough to kill him if she ever caught him cheating. Before when she'd found different numbers in his phone, there was only speculation—no hard evidence; but now she was talking a little reckless. *I really need to just leave and divorce her, but why should I go that route when I'm content with how things are. Shoot, she's gone damn near half of the year.* Nasir rationalized with himself.

I may play this wifey role to the best of my abilities, but his ass doesn't need to forget where I come from. I'm from the projects where shit gets real. Where women chase their man down the street with a butcher knife because they'd caught him—once again—in some shit with another woman, Lorraine thought.

"Looks like you're enjoying your food, your plate's almost empty. Do you want some more?"

"You was right on point with this, it hit the spot. I almost forgot about how good of a cook you are. I haven't had your cooking in so long. You can just put whatever is left up, I'll eat it later."

"You look worn out baby. Why don't you let me give you a massage?" Lorraine made the comment thinking Nasir would've noticed how tired she was as well, and suggest that they give each other a massage; boy was she wrong.

"That's what I'm talking about—come home catering to your man. I like that. I'll be upstairs waiting on the bed when you're finished down here."

Lorraine watched in disbelief as Nasir pushed away from the table, wiped his mouth one last time, and headed out of the dining room. After she finished cleaning up in the kitchen, she made her way up to their bedroom expecting to find a romantic setting since Nasir was so good with those types of things. Normally he would create a sexy ambiance for a romantic evening by just putting on a little music and lighting a candle. But not this time. When Lorraine got to the door of their bedroom, it was cracked just a little and she didn't hear any music playing. She pushed the door open to find him passed out on the bed. Lorraine shook her head, *dang, I knew he was tired, yet he's sitting up there talking about going back out. He's going to keep his behind right here so we can spend some time together while I'm home.* She smiled; watching him sleep in nothing but the silk Armani boxers she'd brought him a couple of weeks ago.

Lorraine went to the bathroom and grabbed a bottle of honey and spice aroma tea therapy oil. Then she got a wash cloth and a small bucket and filled it with warm water and headed back into the bedroom where she sat everything down on the night stand on her side of the bed. She stopped once again, just observing her husband with the thought of him possibly cheating on her still in her mind—she sympathized. *What woman in their right mind wouldn't want my man? His swag is totally different from the average Joe their used to running into. His features pull you in even if you're not trying to be pulled in. His ripped muscles and chiseled physique makes you wet, and not to mention, he has a great career and doesn't mind treating a woman like the queen she is. But he loves me with all of his being; so he couldn't, and wouldn't, cheat on me,* she thought.

She shook the thought out of her head, poured a little oil in the water, and then dipped the washcloth in the water to wet it slightly before rolling it up. She placed the wash cloth on the back of his neck. He was lying in the perfect position on his stomach; she wouldn't have to try and move him for what she had planned. Nasir didn't move an inch. She picked up the oil and let drops drip down his back and then in a slow motion, Lorraine began to rub the oil into his skin, feeling some of the tension in his body leave instantly.

She climbed up on the bed and sat on the back of his legs. Her motions changed to a circular movement which must've felt really good to him, because she heard Nasir's toes crack right after she did it. He smiled in his sleep and then licked his lips. To her, it was no longer about making him feel good, she was now turned on and needed some pleasing of her own. As she watched him enjoy the massage she was giving, she felt the spot between her legs begin to beat, so she nudged him to try to get him to turn over.

"Mmm mmm. . ." was all that came out of his mouth. All the while he still held the slight smile on his face.

Since Lorraine couldn't get him to turn over by nudging him, she decided to take matters into her own hands— literally. She began to fondle his hanging pleasure which she knew would get him excited and in the mood. To her surprise, Nasir was already rock hard. *Damn he's hard and not trying to get any of this? Let's see about that,* she thought.

Nasir was having the best dream of his life and he wasn't trying to be disturbed out of it. The dream included having toe curling, back bending, head-board banging, hot and sweaty sex with none other than Tyquasia. The dream started shortly after he'd fallen asleep.

There was a knock at the door. When he went to answer it there she stood in a floor-length trench coat, a pair of sexy six-inch heels, and a look on her face that said, "fuck me now!"

"Hey baby, I was just about to call you to see what you wanted for dessert," he said moving to the side. "Come on in."

"Dessert huh?! How's this for dessert?" she asked opening and dropping the trench coat to the floor; leaving her standing there in all of her naked glory. "Here's an 'all you can eat dessert' special just for you."

"I swear you make me happy each day that I'm married to you. You never cease to amaze me. That spontaneous shit turns a nigga on."

"I try to do what I can to keep you on your toes. I never want you to get comfortable. I wanna keep us growing so you can never say how it used to be." With those words that Ty spoke, Nasir felt that he didn't have to respond. His

actions were about to speak volumes. He led her to one of the couches in the sunken living room, bent her over the back of one of them and dropped his sweats. Nasir gripped each one of Tyquasia's plump ass cheeks and proceeded to dive in. Ty was on a whole different planet of pure pleasure. He knew exactly what he was doing—what spot to hit and when to hit it.

The pressure that was building up could only be described as an outer body experience because when the orgasm hit Ty, her knees buckled; her body quivered and all the energy she was using to hold on to the couch and throw it back at him was gone. Nasir took that as his cue to finally let loose what he'd been holding in. His motto was to always let his woman get hers first. He never went limp. His manhood was ready for some more action, so he pulled her leg up onto the couch for stability and slid in at a slow pace.

Lorraine pushed Nasir again, this time with force; she was aggravated and horny as hell. She could feel the light moisture between her thighs building. She was ready for her man to unleash his beast on her. Or at least get one of his hellafied tongue lashings, 'cause if nothing else, his head game was Grade A approved.

"Whatchu doing? It was just getting good, damn!" Nasir barked at being snatched from his dream. He opened his eyes.

"I know the massage was getting good, but I'll finish that later. I need you to take care of something else right now." Lorraine purred in a low seductive tone, pulling her maxi dress up and revealing a smooth oasis.

Fuck man, I'm slippin'. She must've thought I was talkin' about the massage being good. Shit, I didn't even feel the damn massage and I'm mad as fuck that she woke me up during the best part of the dream. Shit, why couldn't she wake me up after we were done experiencing each other fully? I had just busted my first nut and Tyquasia had cum hard. We were both ready for the next wave of pleasure to come. I'm amazed at how real that dream felt. It was like my dick was made especially for her pussy or maybe it was the other way around; either way, I have to have her, Nasir thought, drifting back off into his dream.

"Did you hear me?" Lorraine asked watching him as he stared off into space.

"Turn over," he ordered.

"Baby, you know I hate it from the back. Let's just do it how we always do it. You never had a problem with it before," Lorraine replied laying back.

Nasir sighed, "You want missionary? Fine, I'll give you missionary. And like a trained robot, he pushed his chest into hers and inserted his member swiftly. He wasn't pleased at all, he couldn't focus on what he was doing because his mind was on someone else.

Lorraine wasn't feeling it either; as horny as she was, the intimacy wasn't there at the moment. The spark they possessed when their bodies met was usually undeniable that they were made for each other; but this very moment was proving something else.

Damn, maybe I should learn some more tricks. Then again, why should I? He's never wanted anything different before.

The back and forth battle Lorraine was having with herself had taken her fully out of the moment. Lorraine was a square during sex. All she really liked was the missionary position and head. She didn't like to try new things or suck dick. Her older sister called her a sexual bore. She told Lorraine that in order to keep her man satisfied, she would have to go above and beyond what any other woman who didn't have the ring, house or car would do.

Nasir watched Lorraine lay there like a corpse—no moans, movements or anything. His sex tool instantly became soft. He knew then that he was done trying to make his wife explore different things. He pulled out of her, got up and headed to the bathroom. When he looked back at Lorraine she was still lying in the same spot in a daze. She hadn't even noticed that he was no longer in her. He shook his head, locked the bathroom door and started the shower. While in the shower he was lost with thoughts of Tyquasia; he needed to see her tonight. He wanted to hold her, kiss her, touch her and if she would allow it—please her.

Chapter Six

So What Does This Mean?

Tyquasia's mind had been distracted since parting with Nasir that morning. She couldn't focus in her classes, and on her way home she caught herself wondering what he was doing while she was sitting at a red light. She probably would've still been sitting there if it wasn't for the person behind her holding down on their horn, informing her that the light had changed. When she got home she didn't want to do anything; no studying, watching TV or cooking anything. All she wanted to do was lay in bed and wait on his call. He hadn't called all day. She checked her phone a couple of times to make sure it was on and that the volume was turned all the way up.

When her phone started ringing, she immediately dropped her bag containing her books and hurriedly dug through her Hermes bag. She checked the name on the screen only to find that it was Benzino calling from jail again. Ty sighed. *When is that nigga gonna get the picture?* Her once excited mood was gone. She declined the call like she'd done so many times before. She decided a talk with D would probably take her mind off of Nasir. That wasn't the case though, he was on her mind now more than ever.

After talking to D and calming her nerves, Tyquasia

finally relaxed. She basically talked D's ear off about Nasir. D felt some type of way about the new man in Ty's life, so D implemented a little plan. D didn't tell Ty all of the thoughts running through D's mind, but did put a little bug in Tyquasia's ear and she seemed to be all for it. They decided they would start their plan off ASAP.

Ty came back downstairs from relaxing in her room, she needed to get a snack. When she reached the bottom of the stairs, she instantly screwed her face up when she found Khia's suitcase and carryon bag packed and ready to go. Khia sashayed toward the living room, fully dressed, and no longer in her usual lounge-around attire that she would keep all day while in the house. She was eating a bowl of cereal, not paying any attention to Ty, standing there with a confused look on her face. Ty cleared her throat and asked the question that was already evident. "Why are your bags packed? Are you going somewhere?"

"Oops girl, you scared me!" Khia replied jumping, nearly spilling some of the cereal and milk. "I'm going back home. Sabre called me and said that some S.B. boyz been watching my apartment. I can't afford to have my shit broken into, even though there ain't anything in there for them to take except my little ass TV and DVD player. I'm sure they wouldn't fuck with my clothes and shoes unless they're some cross dressers under cover, but I don't want to deal with the damages."

Ty leaned against the wall, arms folded across her chest with a *bitch please* look on her face. Something wasn't right and Ty knew it, she just couldn't quite put her finger on it. "Since when have you been concerned about them Street Banger Boyz running up in yo' shit? If they really wanna run up in your place, they're gonna do it if you're there or not.

Them niggas know you ain't got shit worth taking. What is the real reason you want to go back to Miami so abruptly? If it's about last night, I told you not to worry about that. Paige will get over that shit sooner or later." Ty stepped away from the wall and had a seat on the arm of the couch right across from Khia so that she could get a closer look to see if she was lying or not.

"Ok, you're right. It's not about my place; but girl, Deron done gone and got himself locked up again, so now I gotta go to his mama house and find out what's going on. You know she's old and disabled, so she won't be able to make any of his court dates or put money on the phone. I didn't want to tell you cause I know how you feel about me still having anything to do with him, but I can't help it, I love him." Khia looked in the direction of the muted TV to avoid Tyquasia's disapproving stare.

"I know you didn't just say that nigga's name in my presence. I told you when he got you pregnant, told you he didn't want the baby, and made you get an abortion in the eleventh grade, that you needed to leave his ass alone. Then I told you again when you ended up at the health department 'cause something didn't feel right down there, only to find out that his nasty ass had burnt you with Gonorrhea. He's had two kids in the last two years with two different bitches; and you're still riding for him. When are you going to learn that being a ride or die bitch ain't what it's cracked up to be. At least not with him. Dudes don't respect that. I just can't fuck with you right now; if you wanna leave, come on so I can drop you off at the airport, 'cause I could be doing other shit right now."

Khia wanted to spazz on Ty for the way she was acting,

but she knew Ty was right, and since she couldn't reveal the real reason she was in such a rush to get back home, she went along with Ty and just ignored her attitude. They'd been riding for a little while and Ty still hadn't said one word.

"Look, I know you're mad at me 'cause I can see your top lip all curled up. I was going to ask you if I could hold some money, thinking that we would be parting on a good note. My rent is due at the beginning of the month, ain't no groceries in the house, and the cable man cut my shit off a week before I came up here."

"My lip is not curled, but since you think you know so much, hell yeah I'm mad! It sounds like you're trying to play me Khia. First off, I know you get food stamps and you're barely ever home to watch cable. So I don't know why you're worried about that, not to mention that your rent ain't nothing but thirty dollars a month because you're on Section 8 housing; so who you fooling?" Ty accelerated the gas showing signs that her anger was steady rising.

"You know I'm not working. I really need the money. I'm not going to put any money on Deron's canteen if that's what you're thinking and I promise I'll pay you back."

"I know damn well you ain't gone take my money and put it on that nigga's books even if I didn't make the money. And you've been my friend too long, I know you...your ass ain't gonna pay me back," Ty chuckled and then got right back serious. "Ok, check this out, I'm going to give you the money only because you're my girl and I'm taking your word on this shit, but don't get it twisted, if I find out there's some other shit going on, I'm writing yo' ass off with the quickness. You won't be able to ever ask me for another dime!" Tyquasia made herself very clear while pulling up to the departures area at the airport.

Ty got her purse from the back seat and pulled out a stack of hundred dollar bills. She counted off twenty of them and handed them to Khia. "Don't ever say I ain't never gave you anything. Call me and let me know when you make it home safe."

Khia beamed with excitement as she accepted the money. "Thanks again girl. I want to come back up here in a few weeks once I get everything straightened out and taken care of in Miami, but that's only if you want me to come back."

"Now you know I want yo' crazy ass to come back up here. Just go home, take care of what you have to take care of, and then we'll go from there. I might be down there before you can get back this way anyway. I need to visit my mom."

"True. Alright, let me get going. You see how muthafuckas is starting to look at us crazy 'cause we're holding up the line," Khia giggled.

"Yeah, 'cause I don't want to have to act a fool if one of their asses start beeping at me."

Once Khia had gotten her luggage out of the car, she waved back at Ty and headed inside the airport. Ty pulled off into traffic and headed home. She really needed to be studying right now and since her study partner and friend, Paige, hadn't spoken to her all day, Ty knew it would be a long boring night of hitting the books alone and writing her paper.

* * * * *

Lorraine snapped out of her outer body experience when she heard the front door slam. She got up and made it to the window just in time to see Nasir driving out of their roundabout driveway. She retrieved the house phone from it's cradle and dialed his number. The phone rang a few times and then the voicemail picked up. *What does his ass call himself doing just up and leaving without as much as a "I'll be back soon."* She asked herself questions that only Nasir could answer.

Nasir already knew who was calling the instant his phone began to ring; so instead of answering the call only to argue, he let the phone call go directly to voicemail. After she hung up, he figured it best to cut his phone off completely or her calls would be an ongoing thing until he went back home; so that's what he did.

He drove around for a while with so many thoughts running through his head. This was weird for him because he loved his wife, but he also loved to sleep with other women. What man out here doesn't cheat? He had questions on top of questions that he didn't have the answers to. He'd been with plenty of women, but he'd never connected to one enough to contemplate the ultimate crossover of leaving his wife. He was so used to viewing his wife as his soul mate, that he felt weird now because she was now in his mind and heart as a question mark. *Was their marriage, and their relationship in general, in its final stage or should they try counseling? Maybe Lorraine still doesn't see the bigger issue here,* he thought. *Damn, do I even want help with my marriage? Do I really love my wife if I feel this strongly about a woman I haven't even slept with?*

The reason he'd felt connected to Tyquasia since the first night he'd met her was because she reminded him so much of the old Lorraine. The one that liked to go out, party, drink, meet new friends, explore new oasis, challenge herself to do better and who was not content with where she was in life.

He felt as though Lorraine had changed and had become too comfortable. As the old saying goes, you never get too comfortable in a marriage because, one: your partner will start to reminisce about the way things used to be, and two: your spot will end up substituted with someone who can live up to the things you lack. Ty was young, but he knew she wasn't a content type of woman; he felt that fact every time he was in her presence.

* * * * *

Usually Ty would need a buddy to get through a study session, but tonight she was doing it by herself and for the most part staying focused. Pandora hummed Lyfe Jennings's song, "My Life" through the speakers as she wrote the paper that she hoped would earn her a high grade since it counted for a third of her final grade.

Sounds like the door bell, she said as she hopped out of bed. *I knew my girl wouldn't let me down on a study session. I'm so glad that she came to her senses and got out of that funky rut.*

"Hey pretty lady. Sorry to just pop up on you without calling, but I needed to see you. I was just driving around and figured I'd stop by. I hope you're not busy."

She smiled brightly at the sight of his handsome face and the low sound of his raspy voice. "No, I'm not busy. Come on in. I'm actually glad you decided to stop by seeing as I haven't heard from you since we parted ways this morning. You've been on my mind," Ty said giving him the side eye.

Nasir walked in noticing that all the lights were off. "Were you asleep? I was tired when I got home. I ended up passing out. Believe me, you've been invading my thoughts all day."

"We were up pretty late talking. No, I wasn't sleeping. I was just relaxing. I thought tonight would be my first night staying alone since I moved in here. Wait a minute, how did you get away from your wife?" she questioned raising her right eyebrow.

"What do you mean how did I get away from my wife? I'm a grown ass man. Shit, I just left," he said with a cocky attitude.

"Yeah, aiight Mr. Grown." Tyquasia grabbed his hand and led him up to her bedroom.

Nasir's eyes followed her ass as it swayed up the stairs.

"Were you looking at my ass?" Ty asked hitting him playfully as they reached the top of the steps.

"Who me? Nawh! Why would I do such a thing?" he answered with an innocent smile.

While he checked her nice sized bedroom out, Ty ran over to her bed to remove her books and tablet. *Shoot, I'll study and finish this paper later.*

Nasir saw her putting her books on top of her desk in the corner of the room but didn't say anything about it. He kinda liked it. She was making time for him, something his wife rarely ever did.

"I like your style. It's not so feminine and it has an edge to it. Nice! Did you decorate your condo yourself?"

"Yep, did it all myself. I think you're trying to find anything to talk about other than what matters. What brings you back my way so soon mister? You left my place at noon today to spend time with your wife while she's home and now you're back. What happened?" Ty asked taking a seat on her bed and turning Pandora down just a little.

"It's really nothing that I want to talk about. I came here

'cause I knew you would put me in a better mood, not so I could discuss a prior situation over and over again. I could've stayed home for that. You were steady on my mind even hours after I left," Nasir stated somewhat irritated. He did not mean it to sound as harsh as it did, but the tension from Lorraine was still in him. He sat next to Ty and rubbed his hand over his smooth face with a deep sigh.

"Ok, that's fine. We don't have to talk about what brings you here. I don't even care why you're here, I'm just happy that you are. Are you hungry? I'm a beast in the kitchen," Ty joked making light of their first awkward moment.

"Nawh I ate a lil' while ago. I didn't mean for my words to come out with so much force. I have a lot on my mind. I don't know how to deal with it or what I should do with the things I'm thinking about."

"Well, when you're ready to talk, I'll be here ready to listen. I won't try to pull it out of you. How about we get out of here to do something that will get your mind off of whatever is troubling you? As a matter of fact, I think I have the perfect place that we can go to and let loose."

Nasir had an unsure look on his face. *Oh shit, being in the club talking to women is one thing, but if word got back to Lorraine that I was seen out with another woman her damn head would spend.* He thought long and hard about the repercussions before speaking. "Aiight, we can do that as long as the place is not a club. I see enough of those."

Hmm, he agreed to step out in public with me. He definitely gets a point in my book. I just knew he was going to be apprehensive or better yet, say no. "Trust me, there won't be any clubbing tonight," Ty replied with a slight grin. "Let me just get myself together. It won't take long," she hollered as she high tailed it to the bathroom.

"Women always say it won't take long and it always does. Aye what happened to your girl Khia?"

Tyquasia stuck her shower cap covered head out of the bathroom, "She went back to Miami. She said she had to take care of some business." Ty said before disappearing back inside of the bathroom.

Thirty minutes later Ty was ready to head out to the surprise destination that she had in store for Nasir. But that was not the only surprise Ty had for him. She caught him off guard when she hit the alarm on her car as he was headed to his.

"I'm driving this time. I owe you a ride considering what you did for me and Khia yesterday, so sit back and enjoy the ride." she said as she started up the engine.

Nasir smiled at her as he got in the car. He liked the way she was taking charge of the evening and gave him little, if any, control. He starred out the window as Ty drove quickly through her neighborhood and on a path he did not know. "Since you insisted on driving, I guess that means you don't want me to know exactly where we're going."

"My point exactly," Ty smiled.

"You haven't been here but for a hot second, and yet you're driving around like you run the city. What do you know 'bout this side of town anyway?" Nasir asked as he began to recognize that they were in the part of town he'd grew up in.

"I saw this place when I first got here. It wasn't open at the time because it was early that day, but I asked a friend about it and she said it's a lot of fun." Ty acted as if she was still driving to her location, nearly bypassing her actual location.

Before Nasir knew it, Ty made a sharp right turn into the parking lot of Cascades.

"What do you know about Cascades? This was the place to be on Friday and Saturday nights when I was a teenager," Nasir said with excitement. "Their old school Sunday nights be jumpin' too! I haven't been here in a few years, so this is definitely going to take my mind off of what it's on. I remember my wife and I used to do little fun, spontaneous, things like this back in the day, but then her career became her life. We're going to have some fun."

Tyquasia winced as the words, "my wife" came out of his mouth. *I see I'm going to have to teach him that there are some things you can and can't say around me, and that "wife" word is one of the ones he can't say.*

"Ok, hush and let's go on in before you ruin the fun part by what's coming out of your mouth."

"I caught that. I feel you. I don't want to say that around you and have you feel uncomfortable, so I will try to control that," Nasir said smiling with an ever so sexy smile. His succulent lips spreading, letting his perfect teeth peek through.

They entered the building and began lacing up their skates. Ty lost her balance the first time she tried to stand up. They both laughed and were enjoying themselves. Even though it was Tyquasia's bright idea to go to the skating rink, she hadn't skated since she was a little girl. She was slowly grasping the techniques that Nasir was learning and teaching her at the same time. They went around the rink several times; flirting like teenage lovers and looking like a couple who were very much in love.

Nasir rolled up behind Ty, scaring her enough to the point that she stumbled a bit. He caught her and helped her regain her balance. "Damn, my fault. I didn't mean to scare you, you were just looking so good skating in front of me with these form fitting jeans hugging your ass and showing off that gap between your thighs. When I look at you, I admire your beauty from head to toe," Nasir whispered, moving in close behind her so that he could cop a quick feel.

"I'm just glad you caught me 'cause that would've been an embarrassing ass fall. It probably would have resulted in a pile up as fast as some of these people are skating," Ty giggled. "Now, back to what you were saying about how you admire my beauty from head to toe. That does something to me internally. I want you Nasir. I want you now!" Tyquasia said feeling the heat rise between her thighs.

"I want you just much as much as you want me. Shit, I probably want you more. I think it's time for us to blow this spot. How 'bout it?" He felt his Mandingo rising at the mere thought of entering Tyquasia's treasure.

"Sounds like we're on the same page," she said with a wink.

"Good, I'm driving this time though. You know how many short cuts we could've taken to get here?" he laughed. "I gotta make a quick phone call while you're returning your skates."

Ty's mood immediately changed at the mention of Nasir making a phone call. Her sudden attitude must've shown on her face because he started to explain, "It's not what you think. I need to call and check the voicemail box at the office. I never did forward my calls to my cell phone. I usually always go in the day after an event because press is running high from the coverage at that event. I have to be there to answer questions. My staff is equipped to do it, but I'm a control freak so I prefer doing things myself. I'm not calling Lorraine, so you don't have to worry about that."

"Oh, cause I was about to say…You better tell me something. I'm not at all worried. Shoot, if anyone has something to be worried about, it's her not me," Ty joked, but she was also dead serious and he knew it.

Nasir didn't even reply, he just shook his head. Although he was turned on by her feisty attitude, the question still remained in the back of his head, *Is this how it's going to be between us if we take things a step further or really make something out of the feelings between us?*

After making the phone call that he needed to make, they got in Tyquasia's car and headed to a hotel. The entire ride there Ty was thinking about what could possibly happen when they got in the room. She wasn't nervous, more so excited, that she could finally find out if he was everything she thought he was and if he could live up to how he was in her dreams.

Nasir was ready to get things going. He wasn't thinking about his wife or their marriage; his mind was strictly on sliding in Ty's tunnel. He stared at her occasionally as he drove. Ty loved to show off her 36C, plump, but not too much, breast; and every chance Nasir got he would take a peek at them. *Yeah, tonight's going to be a damn good night,* he thought. When he pulled up to the hotel, he hopped out of the car, tossed the valet the keys and went around to the passenger side to open the door for Ty. She got out of the car and followed close behind him as he stopped at the front desk for a brief moment. When he was done at the front desk, he took her hand and escorted her over to the elevator. Once the doors opened, he inserted the key card into the elevator slot and it began to ascend upward. While they rode, waiting for the elevator to get to the thirty-fifth floor, Nasir rubbed Ty's back, letting his hands move downward and over her ass, cupping it.

"I'm gonna make you feel so good," he said as the elevator reached their floor. When the doors opened, they stepped right into a luxurious presidential suite. Ty took a look around the suite, checking everything from the fully-stocked bar with all top shelf liquors, to the well-designed living room. She moved along on her mini tour and walked into the bedroom. Her eyes lit up. There were rose petals all over the bed, candle light lit up the room with a glow just like the one in her dream. Ty walked further into the room to see a bottle of champagne in a bucket of ice chilling; two flutes sat next to it. She couldn't do anything but smile.

Nasir crept into the room and slid up behind her. "Remember that call I made? This wouldn't have been possible without it. Just a little something I had put together at the last minute," he finished off his statement by kissing her on the neck.

"I love this Nasir. I really do. It's not every day that a woman has things like this done for her. It's things like this that count; not money, cars and jewelry. I didn't know you had pull like this. I guess money talks."

"I guess so," he replied kissing her. Their lips touched as if drawn together like magnets.

Ty eased her tongue in so that he could savor the sweet taste of her tongue. "I want you to give it to me right here and right now. Pay close attention to every part of my body. I want you to treat it like a medium-well steak; savor the flavor in the beginning and by the end it should be devoured." Ty shuddered feeling his member at full length poking at her thigh. It begged to be freed from its enclosure.

That was all he needed to hear as he peeled her clothes off piece by piece. He paid close attention to every part of her skin that was revealed with the absence of clothing. When she was down to just her black lace thong, Nasir spoke, "Your body is amazing!"

Ty stared at him, seeing the fire and hunger in his eyes. While Nasir took his time taking off her clothes, she ripped at his shirt, snatched his belt loose and ripped his pants open. She admired his cut up chest and abs. Nasir had a well-defined body; every rip defined a muscle. She wanted him right then more than she had ever wanted Benzino in their three year relationship.

"Right here and right now I'm committing to giving you the best feeling you ever had before. I'm about to tread the water and when you least expect it, I'm going to dive in it," he said recalling her reaction in his dream when he went in without notice.

Nasir made love to her body, softened her heart, fucked her mind through his actions and twisted her soul; but Ty didn't realize that. She was in a blissful moment with the man she'd had wet dreams about since the very first time they met. He would get her right to the point of being ready to cum and then he would pull back, only to get her to that point once again. It worked in his favor because as he repeated that routine, it only made Ty cum harder. The motions were just right. The union between her treasure to his chest was perfect in every sense. Something that should've been a fuck session quickly turned into a journey of passion. The time was nearing again—from the quivering to the boost of liquid threatening to shoot from her as Nasir dug deeper and deeper with every thrust. His slightly curved at the tip dick repeatedly hit her G-spot at just the right angle. Ty couldn't take anymore, she lost control and her juices flowed from within, making a trail down her thighs and leaving a small puddle under her ass.

"You got a nigga going. Awh...Fuck! Uhhh...shit...This pussy is so good!" Nasir said breathlessly, shuddering as he came long and hard; jerking his body into a stiff hold. He lay there cracking his toes while Ty slid right up under him and laid her head on his chest; listening to the sounds of his heartbeat gradually slowing down. They were both one in the same.

"Mmm...mmm...mmm! That was some of the best sex I've ever had, and judging from your resting eyes and that smile on your face, you agree," Ty said staring up at him.

Nasir rubbed his hand down her bare back. "I must admit you did the damn thang keeping up with me like that." He wrapped his hands around her tightly. "I don't see myself letting you go anytime soon."

"That's just what I wanted to hear because I don't see myself being with anyone else except you." That was the last thing she said before drifting off to sleep.

Chapter Seven

My Business Is Just That, My Business

After tossing and turning all night, Lorraine was in no mood to get out of her bed. But she knew if she missed the brunch date with her sister she would never hear the end of it. Her phone started ringing while it lay right next to her head on the pillow. She lay there staring at the ceiling and grabbed the phone thinking the call was from Nasir.

"Hello!"

"Hey sis, you sound excited to hear from me this morning. I was thinking, why don't I just swing by and get you. That way we can ride to our brunch together and it'll give us more time to talk," Eva said.

When Lorraine heard her sister's voice she closed her eyes and counted to ten; taking a deep breath. "Ok, sure. See you soon," she replied somberly and hung up, not giving her sister a chance to respond. Although she felt awful emotionally, she had to make sure she looked up to par every time she stepped out of the house. Anything less would be unacceptable. She put on a Rachel 'Caroline' Faux wrap dress with a cropped blazer, and settled on a pair of lady-like Louis Vuitton four and a half inch pumps that accentuated her toned legs. Eyeing herself in the full length mirror, she was pleased. She applied her makeup just as Eva pulled up.

"Hey, so where's my little guy?" Lorraine asked expecting to see her nephew strapped in in the back seat.

"After our brief talk yesterday, you sounded like you needed a drink and some girl talk, so I'm here to give you both. Let's go. I left him with Trent so you could have my undivided attention. Miss Diva extraordinaire, you look amazing; better than you sounded on the phone."

"You know no matter how down I am, I would never be caught dead in public looking ratchet. A lot of people crown me a fashionista; so I can't let the people down by allowing some opposing paparazzi catch a shot of me slippin' on my dress code," Lorraine replied.

They arrived at Murphy's and were seated. Once they'd put their drink orders in Eva started up. "You didn't really say too much on the ride over, so let me say my piece before we get deep into our talk," she said taking over like she always did.

I knew this shit was going to happen. It never fails with her. Here she goes with this "let me speak my piece first" shit! Damn, I really don't have anyone that will just sit and listen to me talk for hours when I need it. Why can't anyone just hear me out for a change? I can't talk to my publicist because she's always "business this and business that." My assistant has to stay in an assistant's place. My big sister, Eva, is being the control freak that she is; so I can't talk to her because she's always right. I could never tell her that though, because she is my big sister and I love and adore her. I would never want to hurt her feelings, Lorraine thought as her sister rambled on. She felt herself shutting down. She knew before their conversation started that she would gain nothing from it. She rarely did. This conversation, like so many others, was just more time wasted. Eva often wondered why they rarely saw each other; this was a prime example why.

When they received their drinks Lorraine decided not to order any food. She didn't have much of an appetite. Eva stopped long enough to order herself something to eat, and after she placed her order she went right back into the one-sided conversation she had initiated moments earlier.

"I'm just saying Lorraine, you have what any woman would only wish to have: a successful career; a great, intelligent, successful and sexy husband; no kids and room to make your life grow for the better. The only person that could fuck up all of the good things going on in your life is you. Y'all married young and have been married for a few years now. I don't see anything wrong with him fucking another woman from time to time when he's on the road. Shoot, he hasn't had the chance to live out his young adult life.

You make it even worse by not experiencing different things with your husband. Those things could keep your relationship spicy and poppin', but you refuse to do them. It's amazing that you have a successful career doing something that you love to do, but spending all that time away from him, at this point in your marriage, isn't good. It's like you're begging another woman to come take your place and do all of the things that you're not doing. I know the life span of a model's career isn't long, so you have to get all you can out of it while you can, but you have to compromise some things. Stop being such a workaholic, especially when you don't have to be."

Lorraine couldn't take another word of her sister's so-called helpful talk. "Let me stop you right there. My life is just that—my life. Our mother was a strong woman; she never depended on a man to help pay her bills, put groceries in the house, or anything else for that matter. I'm not going to settle for just sitting at my man's side twenty-four hours a day or vice versa. That's the shit that would force us into divorce. He has his career that he loves. Do you think I would ever ask him to take a step back from it because I wanted more time from him? No, I wouldn't, because to do that would be selfish. Relationships go through rough patches, but only the strong survive and we will survive. Thanks for nothing Eva, I know I can always depend on you big sis," she said sarcastically. "If you want to stay and finish your brunch, I will catch a cab home; but I'm out!" Lorraine said as she started preparing her things to leave.

"Wait Raine. I didn't mean to overstep my boundaries."

It was too late. Lorraine was past the point of continuing their talk. She didn't know if her feelings were because maybe her sister was telling the truth and she just didn't want to hear it, or if she actually felt right in doing what her heart told her to do, which was to stick to her career. But either way, she was pissed. She stopped at the front of the restaurant and asked the hostess to call her a cab and she proceeded outside to wait for a ride.

I don't know why I ever thought she would understand anything that I'm going through. She solves her relationship problems by jumping from one man to another when the one she trusts does her wrong. She's still trying to fill a void because she never had her father in her life. Shit, I'm glad I didn't tell her that Nasir didn't come home last night. That would've been all the ammo she would've needed to make speculations that he was out seeking pleasure elsewhere,

Lorraine thought.

As she paced back and forth outside of the restaurant, Lorraine got on the phone and called her publicist Nancy, who was also her manager. She needed a distraction from all that was going on.

"Hey, great minds think alike. I was just about to call you to run some up-and-coming dates by you for some gigs that I'm in the process of finalizing," Nancy said getting straight to business.

"I need a break, I really do. I'm drained and I haven't been spending much time with my husband; it's really starting to hinder my relationship." Lorraine rubbed her temples as she spoke.

"You know as your manager I'm only trying to do what I think is best for you, and right now, that's taking your career to new heights. You can deal with the other stuff at a later time; as a matter of fact, we're gonna be leaving a couple of days earlier than planned for Fashion Week, just so you can get your mind focused on the business aspect of what we're trying to achieve. Let's not stray away from the plans and goals that we set just a couple of months ago," Nancy said sternly, but meaning it in the most caring way possible.

"Ok, ok, whatever. I get it! I know you only have my best interest at heart, but my mind is clouded right now. Maybe that is what I need to do—step away from the issue so that I can see it in a different light and then come up with a way to fix it. When do I need to be ready to go?"

"I'm checking flight times now. I'll text you with the time; just be ready to roll in the morning. That's a great way to look at things. I just knew you were going to fight me tooth and nail about heading out earlier than expected. You will have time to rest before New York's Fashion Week, right now our destination is Philadelphia; they have a great gig waiting for you there. Everything is going to be ok. We got this!"

"Sounds like fun. I hope you're right and everything really does turn out ok. Talk to you later."

"I love you girl, get some rest and remember...no stressing; stress lines show up in pictures."

Lorraine had been riding in the cab for most of her conversation with Nancy. When she first got in the cab, instead of telling the driver where she was going, she wrote her address on a piece of paper and gave it to him so that she could concentrate on her phone call. As the cab pulled around the driveway to the front door of her home, she noticed that Nasir still hadn't come home because his car wasn't there. She paid the driver, took a deep breath, shook all of her ill feelings and doubts from her head, and headed inside to pack for the two weeks she would be gone. As she gathered her things she decided that the most she planned to do was to inform Nasir that she would be flying out on business earlier than expected. That would just take a simple note; she refused to worry herself with calling him.

Chapter Eight
Can't Be Trusted

The night that Khia arrived back in Miami she put her plan into action. What Tyquasia didn't know at the time that she dropped Khia off at the airport is that when she walked Nasir out to his car, her cell phone started vibrating and it just so happen that it was sitting right next to Khia on the couch. At first Khia was going to ignore it, but curiosity got the best of her so she picked it up and saw that it was someone calling from an unknown name, unknown number which Khia knew could only be a jail call since Ty had been complaining about an unknown name unknown number calling her constantly. She recalled Ty telling her that anytime it appeared on her phone she knew it was Benzino. A smile appeared on her face. She answered the phone and ran over to the window looking out toward the parking lot. As she waited for the call to connect she saw Ty and Nasir in an intimate embrace. Khia knew she didn't have much time, so she acted fast. She hit the number one button and was connected to Benzino.

"Hello, hello! Why the fuck have you been dodging my calls this entire time? You do know that I'm going to get out of here and find your ass, and when I do bitch…you better have said all of your goodbyes to everyone you know and love!" Benzino blared through the phone.

"Benz, calm down. This is Khia baby. Why haven't you

called me since you've been locked up? I've been so worried about you," Khia said in a childlike voice.

"Khia, sweetheart what are you doing with Tyquasia's phone?" He asked his question calmly, knowing it was his only chance to get some information on Ty's whereabouts.

"Oh, she flew me to Atlanta to checkout..." Her words became caught up when she realized she'd fucked up by revealing Tyquasia's whereabouts.

"So, you mean to tell me that bitch took my money and moved to Atlanta to start a brand new life? She thinks she can just forget about me like I'm a muthafuckin' after thought? I'm going to kill that little bitch! Khia...listen to me and listen to me good, I want you to get on the next flight leaving out of that fucker. I'm going to set you up a visitation for tomorrow evening and you better be here; remember...I know where you live and I can get you touched."

Khia knew Benzino and she knew he wasn't playing at all. "I promise daddy, I'll be there tomorrow evening. I'm going to come up with something to tell Ty. Oh shit! I gotta go here she comes."

"Yeah, just remember what the fuck I said."

"I know baby. See you soon."

Nasir was getting in the car backing out and Ty was standing there watching him leave. Khia needed just enough time to scroll through Tyquasia's phone so that she could delete the last incoming call. Once she'd done that successfully, she put the phone back where she found it. Khia started up the stairs when she heard the front door open. "Ty, I'm going back to sleep, I don't think I should've eaten that banana; my stomach is in knots. I'll chat with you after your class." She finished quickly before she shut and locked the room door.

See what little Ms. Tyquasia, who thought she had it all figured out, didn't know was that before she and Benzino hooked up, Khia used to fuck Benz from time to time. She had him long before Ty came into the picture. But things between Khia and Benz slowed down after they had a threesome; everything was going just fine until Khia thought she saw Benzino touch the other man's ass. She was in the middle of doing and getting what she loved to do and get, which was sucking one nigga off while getting it doggy style by Benz. Every time she thought about it, Khia tried to tell herself that her eyes had deceived her, but all she could go by was what she saw at that moment. Whether it actually happened or not, what she saw took Khia out of the mood for their sexual game, so she faked a stomach ache and went home. The weird thing was that the dude, Chris, didn't leave when she did. She found out later that Chris was Benzino's lawyer and they had to talk about some business. At least that was the story she was told at the time. Khia still questioned herself, even to this very day, about what she saw and what actually happened.

Khia and Benz had an ongoing relationship. They continued to fuck while he and Ty were together. Their relationship dated back to high school when Khia had gotten pregnant and had to have an abortion; of course she could've had Benzino pay for it without a second thought, but she would've run the risk of him not fucking with her anymore after that, so she blamed her pregnancy on the other dude she was fuckin' and made him pay for the abortion instead of the real father—Benz.

* * * * *

Khia wore form fitting Seven7 Jeans and a V-neck top that wasn't too low cut. She had been on visitations at the jail before and she knew what the clothing restrictions were. Her heels clicked on the pavement as she stepped off of the bus at 6:57 p.m. She made it to the visitation line at 7:00 p.m. on the dot. Benzino walked in, along with a number of other inmates, and the biggest smile appear on Khia's face. Something about the sight of him always gave Khia a special feeling. Benzino filled out his orange jail house jumper. She could tell he'd been working out because of how ripped his arms were. He had grown a little fro which was trimmed up neatly with a nice line up. Just the site of him made the space between her legs start to cream. It was as if he had a permanent hold on her kitty. Benz wasn't smiling at all. He had a stone cold look on his face which told Khia that he was in business mode and she better put the personal feelings to the back burner, at least for her current visit.

"You look good Daddy."

Benz sat still for a while starring at Khia and then he finally spoke, "I'm gonna give you this shit straight and then you can make up your mind how you want to approach me. You can tell the truth and ride on my side, or lie and get the same fate as that little thieving fake ass bitch friend of yours." He paused long enough to make sure that his anger didn't stop him from getting his message across. "The undercover cop that arrested me was a dirty narc. When I got my first court date for this bogus charge, I thought I would be headed up the road to do God only knows how many years; instead I got hit with information on that dirty cop that arrested me.

I gave that information to my lawyer and basically now the whole precinct is under investigation. The judge didn't see a reason for me to sit in jail until the investigation was over, so he sentenced me right then and there. I remember his words, 'It must be your lucky day. I'm sentencing you to five months in jail for those traffic violations and the fifteen parking violations. The drug charge has been thrown out and you're lucky because you could've been going to prison for a very long time.' When I heard those words from the judge, I knew my prayers had been answered. I had already made up my mind on what I was going to do when I got out. I planned on marrying Tyquasia, moving us out of Miami and investing in a legitimate business; probably even letting her go to school like she'd been wanting to do. All that shit went out of the window when the bitch stole my money and moved to another state to start a new life without me. I got something for her though…just wait and see. I have four months left in this hell hole; but *now* when I get out I want *us* to start a new life—me and you. But that will only work if you're willing to ride with me on this. Did you do everything that I told you to do?"

Khia sat there astonished by what Ty had told her, she thought that Benzino had gotten close to a life sentence. *Damn, she must've left soon as this nigga got locked up. Fuck that…I need to ride with him. I know what he's capable of and maybe he'll finally realize that I'm 'that bitch' that he needs to be with,* Khia thought.

"Yes, I'm riding with you. I've always been here for you, you just never seem to acknowledge that. I'm so happy that you won't be spending years and years behind those bars. I did everything that you told me to do," she replied with a long silent sigh.

"I knew that's what you would say. Ok, back to what I was saying. I'll be up out this bitch in four months. During these next four months I need you to find out everything you can on Ty. Her address, hang out spots, any friends she has, who she's fucking, where that nigga lives and who his family is. I need all of that. The first week of every month I need you to have yo' ass here for visitation. In the last week of the fourth month, I want to see you twice; once at the beginning and once at the end. Get to it! Nothing else needs to be said." Benzino finished the conversation and signaled to the guard that he was ready to head back. He looked down at Khia one last time and through gritted teeth he said, "Don't fuckin' play me Khia or you'll wish—like that bitch—you hadn't."

What the fuck did I get myself into answering the damn phone that day? Khia wondered as she walked aimlessly to the bus stop across the street from the jail.

G STREET CHRONICLES
A NEW URBAN DYNASTY
WWW.GSTREETCHRONICLES.COM

Chapter Nine

This Is My Life

Tyquasia and Nasir woke up the next morning around noon; still naked and sticky from the events that unfolded the night before.

"Come on baby, let's take a shower together. I've already missed my morning class and your meeting isn't for a few hours; can you really go home smelling like me? All I smell on you is Amber Romance, D & G Light Blue cologne and sweat."

"Fasho. Let's take a shower. I must warn you, I like my water damn near scolding hot. It just makes me feel extra clean."

"We're on the same page 'cause I was just about to ask you if you're ready to feel a layer of your skin peel off," Ty giggled.

Damn another point for Ty. Lorraine hates extremely hot water, Nasir thought.

"I see someone's happy to see me this morning," she said lightly, tugging at his extended member. "Follow me."

Nasir grabbed a condom off of the dresser. This was the most excitement he'd had from a woman he was interested in a while. Usually, with the women he fucked with, there was never an emotional attachment; just an agreement between two consenting adults. Most of the time when it came to sex it was usually a "one and done" type situation. He never wanted to keep fucking the same woman because she would usually have her feelings involved by the second time and that wouldn't be healthy for his home situation.

He stepped into the shower where Ty was already lathering up. "Took you long enough. I was starting to think this would be a solo mission," she said running her hands along her erect breast.

"I would never leave you hanging," he replied lathering himself up with a wash cloth.

Tyquasia was turned on to a higher level. She pulled the detachable shower head from the wall and ran the water on her sensitive area. She turned the water up to full blast which sent the water shooting out of the shower head on to her pearl, which was peeking out of its hidden oasis. Ty let out a moan as she felt her clit harden immediately. She closed her eyes and moved her hand down over her nipples, pass her pierced belly button, and ultimately to her clean, shaved pussy. Without a second thought, she slowly inserted a finger. She imagined how turned on Nasir probably was watching her pleasure herself.

Nasir couldn't bear to watch her another moment without joining in on the action. He dropped down on one knee and lifted her leg over his shoulder. He took her hand from her opening and dove right in with his tongue. Ty was surprised when he reinserted her finger, this time from the back. She was so close to her climax; she could feel throughout her body, right down to the balls of her feet. Her legs began to shutter and become weak. Nasir held her up as best he could as he finished up the job. He felt her warm juices squirting; they'd just made magic together.

Ty had to sit down on the bench that was built into the

wall of the bath tub. Her legs continued to shake. *That shit was even better than last night,* she thought.

"If you keep on making me cum like that I'm going to have to make that wife of yours disappear," she joked. "Now bring my 'Big Daddy' on over here to me." she said as she used her index finger to coax him over.

Nasir smiled. The sex was great, but that wasn't what made him realize that she was all he wanted wrapped up in one woman. He never knew there was a woman out there with everything in her that he wanted and more. Nasir walked right up to Ty with his pelvic area right at her level, his member pointing at her. She took it and wrapped her warm, wet mouth around it and went to work.

"We may be able to arrange that," he said between grunts.

Ty didn't know what he was talking about so she continued to blow his mind.

"We may be able to arrange that." He repeated and then added, "...making my wife disappear."

Tyquasia stopped sucking and let his dick fall out of her mouth as she held it open looking up at Nasir with his head tilted back.

"What the fuck are you doing? Finish me off baby," he said, head still tilted. When Ty didn't oblige, Nasir grabbed his joy stick and finished the job himself. He turned his back to her, washed up and got out of the shower—heated.

Ty finally had the strength to stand to finish off her shower. When she walked into the sleeping area of their suite, Nasir was sitting on the bed putting on his shoes as if he was preparing to leave.

He looked at her. "You know I was just kidding, the same way you were when you said it. I wanted you to spend the day with me, but maybe that's not such a good idea," he said grabbing his keys off of the night stand.

"Wait Nasir, I didn't know you were just playing from the way you said it. You seemed serious. We're still getting to know each other, so I have to learn when you're just playing and when you're serious. I would love to spend the day with you, but I have two classes later on today; one at 4:45 and the other at 8:30 tonight."

"You can miss them for just one day can't you? You've already missed your morning class, so I think you should just take the whole day off and start fresh tomorrow. I want to learn more about you."

"What will your wife…" She stopped herself mid-sentence. "Never mind. Ok, I'll take the day off. Only this one time though. I can't be doing this on the regular. My semesters here aren't cheap; I have to pass them all."

"I'm sure you will pass them and don't worry about paying for them, I'll pay for your semester."

"It's already done, but you can pay for my next semester." She said smiling and half way joking.

"Consider it done," he said with a wink.

And he didn't ask how much it cost or hesitate to say he'll pay it. I like that, Ty thought.

* * * * *

The last couple of days had been magical for Tyquasia. She'd been going to her classes, but not paying attention in them. Everything reminded her of Nasir. When they weren't together they would spend hours at a time texting and sending each other pictures. From what Nasir told her, he hadn't talked to his wife since she left on her business trip, which was all good with Ty. That gave her plenty of time to claw her nails deep in him and leave her mark. Ty had already coined Nasir as hers; the only dilemma was making that statement a fact vs. fiction.

Ty was on her way home from her afternoon class when she got a call from Khia. She answered right before it could go to voicemail. "Hey girl, it's been a couple of days. I thought for sure you would've called me at least once since you've been back home. I did get your text letting me know that you landed, at least you do follow partial directions," Ty said sarcastically. "I have so much to tell you."

"I know girl. I was supposed to have called. I was just so busy trying to get myself together. I just really want to better myself. You're going to be proud of me. What do you have to tell me? Spill it bitch; you know I'm nosey," Khia said popping her gum right into the phone. She was trying to avoid talking about the real purpose of her phone call.

"What I need to talk to you about can wait, it's too much to try to explain over the phone. Plus I want to see your face when I tell you what I have to tell you. Anyway, what are you up to? It's obvious that your apartment wasn't burglarized as you said it would be since I don't hear you crying and all that."

"No, my apartment wasn't broken into funny ass, but the point is it could've been. These niggas in the hood be watching. They know if they see no movement at an apartment for a certain amount of time that the person is out of town. Knowledge like that gives them every opportunity to break in and take ya shit. I'm not up to much though; I've taken care of my business and I'm ready to come back to the ATL and hang out with you."

"I done told you ain't nobody round there gone break in yo' shit. I mean...for what? They don't have a reason, incentive or a motive. I told you before, just because the opportunity presents itself doesn't mean a person is going to go through with it. I'll be coming down there next week to visit my mother and see how she's doing. You can fly back with me then. Oh yeah, before you start...Paige and I have talked about the little situation between the two of y'all. I told her if either of you are going to be in my life, y'all will respect each other, be cordial toward each other, and get along, or at least act like you do. Shit, it's not like I'm asking y'all to be best friends. Y'all are both my friends so y'all will be around each other whether you like it or not. So save all that attitude shit for the bitches you don't like down there in the projects, 'cause ain't no beef this way; got me?"

I'm over here worried about what the fuck Benz is going to do to her ass when he gets a hold of her, and she's over there making up with a fake-ass, certified, whack bitch. Ok, game on! Khia thought.

"You know what...you're right; ain't no beef. But you let that bitch know if she ever puts her hands on me again, I'm going to cut them muthafuckas from her wrist. Now you can take that as a joke—shit, she can too—but tell her to try me and see," Khia said, her pressure rising and anger building up all over again.

"All that ain't even necessary. Like I told you before, y'all both had too much to drink that night, but you were out of line Khia. I probably would've popped yo' ass too if you were coming at me with a six-inch heel in your hand. We'll talk later, I gotta get home and get dressed for my dinner date."

"For your dinner date? Girl, what dinner date? And with

who?"

"Haven't I told you about your nosiness before? If you must know, I have a dinner date with *my man,* Nasir," Ty replied very matter of fact like.

Khia started coughing. "Damn girl you almost made me choke on my gum with that one. Your man…really? I see what you've been up to while I've been gone, you little whore you. When his wife finds out she's gonna body bag both of y'all. She may not look like it, but a woman scorned will do some evil shit!" Khia warned.

"Pause! When the fuck did you become the spokesperson for their marriage? Yeah, so what they're married! Marriage doesn't always equal happiness. I shouldn't have to explain this to you given how many married men you've fucked in the past. You can miss me with that shit!" Ty snapped.

"Key word that you mentioned is, '*fucked.*' I wasn't trying to be wifed down by no married man, and I damn sho' wasn't running around callin' them 'my man.' Whatever girl…do you. You're grown, handle your business."

"Yeah, 'cause after they fucked you the first time, there never was another time," Ty whispered under her breath. "I'm gonna go 'cause you fuckin' up the mood way up here. I'll holla atchu tomorrow," Ty said ending the call before Khia could even get the chance to respond.

Chapter Ten

A Philly Connection

Nasir was really showing his ass, another night had went by without him coming home. Lorraine couldn't worry herself with his foolishness, she left him a note informing him of her departure and explained that she would be too busy to talk, so he didn't need to call her while she was away. That was really just to spite him. She would be busy, but not so busy that she wouldn't have time to talk to her husband, but that was before all of the recent bullshit he was pulling.

The morning that Lorraine arrived in Philadelphia she didn't have anything planned. Nancy set her up a relaxing day which was exactly what she needed. After dropping her bags off at her hotel, her driver took her down on Market Street so that she could do some shopping. Lorraine brought everything she wanted, then she checked with the driver to see where they would head to next. He informed her that she was set for an all-inclusive spa appointment that was scheduled for 4:30 p.m. She hated to be late to appointments so she told him to head straight there and take any short cuts necessary.

The three-hour spa stay had her feeling as if she was floating on air when she walked. She felt refreshed; not only on the outside, but on the inside as well. Her last stop of the day was supposed to be at a restaurant to have dinner with Nancy. But her thoughts were suddenly filled with Nasir as she scrolled through her phone and came across a picture of the two of them smiling; obviously very happy. Now she wondered what he was doing at that very moment.

"Harold, that's ok. You can turn the car around and take me back to my hotel. I won't be eating out tonight. I'll just call for room service."

"Are you sure Mrs. Cruz? I can have you at the restaurant before your 8:00 reservation."

"I'm sure. I'm really not up for it."

"Ok, right away then."

* * * * *

"Today you will be speaking to teenage, at risk girls who are on the road to becoming a product of their environment. Their guardians will also be present to take in some of this knowledge you're about to drop on their children. With these girls you really have to keep it real raw and uncut; that's the best way to handle them, and I think you can do that just by telling your story. If anything will open their eyes that will."

"If it will put one of these young girls on the right track I will tell them my story."

The promoters for the speaking engagement really did their job in promoting the event, because the community center that sat in the center of one of the roughest parts of Philly was jam packed with teenage girls and their guardians. It was evident that some were there by force. However, whether by force or by voluntary attendance, they would all get something out of what Lorraine was getting ready to speak about.

She walked up on the small stage and cleared her throat. "Hello everyone, I'm honored to be here to speak to all of you today. Thank you for coming out. I want to start off by stating I am not better than anyone in this room. I've had to fight my way to be respected, and when I say, 'fight' I don't mean physically; I mean I went out in the work field to show and prove that I deserved recognition. Today I am going to tell you all my story of struggle, pain, fight and triumph. At any time while I'm talking if you have a question, please don't be afraid to ask; no matter how small it may be. Remember, there's no such thing as a stupid question."

Lorraine took a second, cleared her throat, and began, "I was born to a young girl who was probably the same age as you when she had me. In that instant, her life was over. It was no longer about her anymore, it was now all about my five-year-old sister and me. In the beginning, my mother tried her best to take care of us with only the help of the benefits she got from the State. There wasn't really much she could do for us since we lived in the worst ghettos in the ATL. Her mother, who was also a young teen mother, told her when she found out that she was pregnant for the second time, that there was no way she would help her. She told her that she'd lost her young adult years taking care of her, and she wasn't about to lose her adult years taking care of her grandkids and a fast-tail daughter who didn't want to listen when she'd warned her about street life. By the time I was six months old, my mother, who was seventeen at the time, spent most of her days sitting around me smoking and drinking. A living situation which in turn, caused me to get bronchitis.

When I turned a year old, my mother was strung out on

dope and CPS removed me from her custody and from my grandmother's house. My grandmother came to her senses and decided to keep my sister when the State came to take us. She said she couldn't take us both, but she would be sure to look after one of us. She kept my sister and let me go. They sent me to live with my grandmother's sister Patty. She was the sweetest old woman you could ever meet. My mother would come by a couple times a month to see me, but from what Patty told me she was never in her right state of mind.

Fast forward a few years. At the age of seven—that's right, that's how many years I went without my mother— Patty got sick and was no longer able to care for me. When that happened, my mother went into a drug rehab program that set her up with an apartment, child care and a guaranteed job once she successfully completed the program. She got her act together and it didn't take long for her to follow all of the requirements put on her in order for her to get her children back.

When we were returned to our mother, my sister and I were living with a woman who we knew was our mother, but we didn't actually know her at all. Adjusting to that life was hard. By the time I was nine, my mother was off of the assistance program and in a nice three bedroom apartment, working two jobs and still home in time to make sure that I'd done my homework. On my thirteenth birthday my mother surprised me with a photo shoot. It was only a test run for a local woman's clothing line that she'd designed for teenage girls. At the time, I was really into fashion and taking pictures, I still am of course. From that shoot the organizers of the clothing line loved my pictures and a few weeks later I was called back in to do an official shoot. From there a man in the modeling and entertainment field contacted the woman who designed the line. He told her he needed to find the girl who was posing in her ads. Once he explained his job title as a talent scout to her, she contacted my mother and we met with him. I've been signed with major modeling agencies ever since.

The moral of my story is no matter where you come from, what hand your life is dealt or what someone tells you, you can do whatever you put our mind to. Shoot, have y'all seen our president? Yes, he's black! Who would've ever thought that was possible? To me that sets the stage for all of you, you are the future. There will be a female president one day and I just want to know will it be you, you, you or you? You all have the power to change the stigma that if you come from the projects you won't amount to anything. That's a lie and y'all have what it takes to prove that it's a lie. Oh yeah, and that curse that was going on where every female ended up having a child as a teenager—was broken with me. Here I stand twenty-four years young, from the projects, and with no children. It ended with me. Let it end with you too."

The room erupted in applause. Telling her story had taken a lot out of her, but Lorraine stayed for another hour taking questions from both guardians and teenagers. They thanked her for telling her story because no one had ever made it out of the projects and came back to tell them they could make it too. She'd empowered the mothers to be more present in their daughter's lives. She opened their eyes to the fact that it all started with them.

When she finished taking pictures, signing autographs and giving out, "Reach 1 Teach 1 shirts", Lorraine was getting ready to leave out of the side exit when someone called her name. She turned around and came face to face with the most gorgeous man she'd ever seen in her life. He was standing with a girl who couldn't have been older than fifteen years old.

"Uh, hello! Did your daughter not get a shirt?" Lorraine asked.

"Oh Samyra isn't my daughter; she's my niece. We don't live on this side of Philly anymore, but I thought being here would be good for her. She talks about you so much and I didn't even know who you were, so I just had to come meet you myself." The voice that came from the person standing in front of Lorraine was deep and gruff with a touch of softness to it. When Lorraine further inspected the person she'd originally thought was a man, she realized it was not a man at all. The person speaking to her was a woman who, at first glance, would be presumed to be a man because she was dressed in male attire and had very small breast which could be mistaken for a well-toned man's chest.

"I'm sorry I thought that. . .well, I wasn't paying attention. . ." Lorraine stumbled over her words.

Samyra started laughing, "Auntie you always have the women confused. You even confused Lorraine. Awh man!"

"Yes, I am a woman. My name is Dominique, but my friends call me Dom. Nice to meet you Lorraine," Dom said cracking a smile.

"Samyra go stand over there and let me talk to Lorraine real quick."

"But, she's my…" Dom gave her a look and she must've known what it meant because she walked over to where she was told to and stood there without saying a word.

Lorraine had to stop herself from staring for the second

time. "I thank you for bringing your niece. I'm sure she took at least one thing from my speech and story."

"Samyra commented on just about everything you had to say up there, so I know for a fact that she was listening and took something from your speech and story. I also want to thank you for sharing your story. If you don't mind me asking… how long will you be staying in Philly? I wanna take you out for dinner." Dom watched Lorraine's facial expressions change at the mention of being taken out to dinner by her.

Lorraine was unsure whether or not to accept Dom's invitation. Even though somewhere deep inside she wanted to accept it; she just couldn't. She still didn't know if Nasir was cheating and if he was, she'd convinced herself that playing get back at him with a woman wouldn't have done anything but turn him on.

"I tell you what…I have a very hectic and busy schedule while I am here, but give me your email address or a number where you can be reached, and if I get a free moment I will contact you and let you know if I'm free to take you up on the dinner invite."

"I'll take that. It's better than just a flat out no." Dom reached in her pocket and pulled out her wallet. Lorraine reached out for Dom's business card that held all of her contact information on it. "Listen, really get at me; you hear me?" She said while they both held on to her card. "Who knows, it might be a new beginning for the both of us. I see the ring on your finger, but I also see the unhappiness in your face. What real man would let their beautiful wife walk around looking miserable, putting on a fake smile while in public just to make it seem like home is taken care of when it's really not. I see through that."

Sweat instantly covered Lorraine's face. Had it been that obvious to see all of that even through the smile she tried to keep plastered on her face? What Dom said was the truth. She didn't realize she'd just exposed her whole spot.

"We're not going to indulge into the private affairs of my home life. I have your card and I'll even give you one of mine which only has my email address and business line. I will contact you if I get some free time. Now, I've got to get going." Lorraine said as she turned her attention to Dom's niece who was anticipating what she was getting ready to say to Lorraine once she got the chance to talk to her again. It was obvious by her face that she was a big fan of Lorraine. She motioned for Samyra to come back over to them and the girl did a full out sprint in the short distance between them.

"What do you want to do when you graduate high school?" Lorraine asked Samyra once she caught her breath.

"I really want to be a high fashion model; but coming from where I come from, even though I'm not there anymore, I don't see my dream coming true," Samyra said honestly.

Lorraine looked over at Dom as if she was contemplating something and then she said, "Mmm hmm. When I asked you what you wanted to do after you graduate from high school, you answered my question and then added, 'but'... there aren't any 'buts' when you speak of a dream, goal or your future. You find a way to make them your reality. Just by looking at you I can see that you have all of the potential to be a great model. You're beautiful. I will do what I can to get you there. That's my word. It's not going to be easy, you're going to have to work hard and keep your grades up while doing it. I want you to think of college in your future as well. If you can do those things, then I will help you."

Samyra had the biggest smile on her face, she was showing off all of her top and bottom teeth. Her eyes were big and sparkling, like a kid coming downstairs on Christmas morning.

"Oh my God! Thank you so much. You don't know what this means to me. I can't thank you enough. Yes, I will do everything that you said and I will go above and beyond that to make everything perfect," she said yelling in excitement. She rushed over to Lorraine to give her a hug.

"Alright missy," Lorraine said.

"Dom, I will be in contact with you very soon with further information. I've got to get going," Lorraine said looking at her Michael Kors rose gold watch. She extended her hand. "It was nice to meet you." She rushed off through the exit to the awaiting town car. For some reason she made sure to take her time getting in the car. She could feel Dom staring at her.

Dom watched her the whole way until she disappeared inside her waiting car. *Mission accomplished,* she thought as she opened up her hand to read the card with all of Lorraine's contact information that she'd just placed in her hand before running off.

"You didn't even want to come here and you complained the whole time she was speaking; but now you want to be a *high fashion model* like her?" Dom asked while holding up air quotes to emphasize the term.

"Well, shit! Meeting her up close and in person changed my thought process. She's not bougie like I thought she was. Shoot, she actually wants to take a chance on me and help me, so of course I'm not going to turn it down," Samyra replied.

"So I guess that means I don't have to give you that two hundred dollars I promised you for coming with me?" Dom asked.

"Oh no, I still want my money. I'm going to the mall to get a couple of fly outfits for school next week. Auntie, I wanna know what your plans are for Mrs. Cruz. She really is a nice lady."

"You don't need to worry about all that. Just continue playing your role and you will continue to get paid," Dom said as they got in her 2012 Cadillac Escalade EXT truck.

Chapter Eleven

I Hate What I have To Do

K hia sat in her living room watching Maury and eating a Cuban sandwich from the corner store. Right when Maury was about to reveal the results of a paternity test, someone started banging on Khia's door.

Shit! Now who the fuck is that? A can't even watch my show without being interrupted, she thought.

"Who is it?" Khia yelled stalling so that she wouldn't miss the results that Maury was about to reveal.

"It's Roneeka! Open the muthafuckin' door. I bet yo' ass is in there watching Maury and you probably done already seen that episode. He ain't the baby daddy!" Roneeka yelled back through the door laughing.

Khia slung open the door and high tailed it back to the couch only to see that the show had gone to a commercial break.

"You're so damn rude; you ain't got no manners at all. Is that a Cuban? Can I get a piece?" Roneeka said as she plopped her feet up on the coffee table.

"Remember I'm rude, meaning I'm not sharing shit! I'm surprised you're out of the house anyway after James beat yo' ass, blacked both of yo' eyes, busted yo' lip and fractured one of your ribs for dippin' yo' sticky finger in his stash of money so that you could buy an outfit for the Rick Ross party. When you called and told me that while I was in ATL, I couldn't believe it. You done did some dumb shit in the past, but stealing from yo' crazy ass boyfriend is suicide. I see ya eye and lip are healing up well. The real question is how does that rib feel?"

Roneeka is a chick from around the neighborhood that went to high school with Ty and Khia. She was a cool chick; her only flaw was that she loved to gossip. The girl couldn't hold water if she was suffering from dehydration. Khia liked to hang with her because they were one in the same.

Roneeka, Ty and Khia used to all be the same until Ty got with Benzino and started acting like she was better than them because a nigga upgraded her. Before she got with him they would all wear the same kind of clothes: Baby Phat or the knock off brand Baby Girl, Lot29 and Echo. They would shop at Walmart, Kmart or Target, and they would switch their clothes up between them to make it look like they spent a lot of money when they really hadn't.

She was the tallest and biggest out of the three of them; standing at 5'10" and weighing 175 pounds. The weight filled out well with her height, but it still bothered her that she was always the biggest out of them.

"Mind your damn business Khia. I'm just fine," Roneeka said as she rubbed over her side wincing in pain.

"Mmm hmm. If you say so."

"James didn't fuck me up that bad this time. Anyway, I didn't come over here to talk about that. I've been calling you for the last five days and you haven't answered the phone. Why is that?"

"I had stuff to take care of, damn!" Khia was irritated by

the inquisition.

"It don't look like you're taking care of shit now. I just called you thirty minutes ago and didn't get an answer. I wanna know what happened after you talked to Benz on Tyquasia's phone. I see you're back at home, so that means you did what he told you to do. My question now is, where do you go from here? What did he say when you went to see him?"

"Girl, I've been over here stressing the hell out honestly. You know there are not too many bitches that I talk to about my personal business, so you better keep yo' big ass mouth shut. This nigga wants me to set Ty's ass up." Khia said. She looked worried.

"What do you mean, 'set her up?' Didn't that nigga get like fifteen years? I know he won't be able to touch her physically, but he can put the order in to them Killa Boyz to off her."

"See that's the thing, niggas is out here sleeping and thinking that Benzino got all those years; but he didn't. The narc that arrested him and tried to stick him with the drug charges was a dirty cop. Which means those charges had to be dropped. Benz is only doing some petty jail time and will be out in a couple of months. He wants me to set Ty up; if I refuse to, I will end up getting the same fate that he's going to give Ty, if not worse. On the bright side of things, he said that if I ride with him, and for him on this, we will finally be together; just me and him without all of the extra chicks on the side."

"Uh huh, are you crazy? You can't set our girl up. We done did some scandalous shit in the past together, and even though Ty and I aren't speaking right now, you can't just make her a sitting duck for a nigga to get caught, especially when you have what it takes to at least warn her. That's going against the girlfriend code. I don't care what kind of threats Benz was issuing or any promises he made, you can't go through with that shit because it's going to end up falling back on you."

"I know the code and all that other shit, but right now I'm in a situation where it's me or her. I'm damn sure not choosing her. I know you're going to look at me real sideways right about now, but I actually wanna be with Benz. Regardless if this would've went down or not, I think we still would've been together." Khia spoke as if she were in lala land.

"If my rib wasn't hurting me right now I would smack the shit out of you and hope that some sense comes through. I'm up out this bitch! Call me when you get your mind together and not before."

"Yeah, whatever! If you were in my position you would do the same thing." Roneeka was walking out of the front door when Khia said that statement.

* * * * *

"Hey girl, I'm finally in town. I'm at my mother's place right now. Once I get done talking to her, I'm gonna come pick you up so that we can get something to eat and probably go shopping," Ty said.

"Shoot, I wanna go shopping with y'all too," Diane said.

"Ma, get out of my conversation! Hold on Khia, let me take you off of speaker phone."

"Yo' mama is so crazy. That sounds good to me. I'll start getting ready now."

"Yeah, you do that 'because you know damn well your ass takes forever," Ty replied.

"No longer than the queen of late herself. Mmm hmm,"

Khia joked as they hung up.

Ty was starving and since her mother hadn't cooked anything she decided that getting something to eat would be their first stop.

"I didn't tell you ahead of time 'cause I already knew that you would be mad, but Nasir is in town too. He's hosting a party and I think it's only right that we show up and show out with our fly asses." Ty said as she looked at the menu.

"Oh, so you thought by telling me that we were going out, it would make me overlook the fact that Nasir is here at the same time that you're here. That only leads me to believe that the real reason you're here is because he's here and you thought you could kill two birds with one stone. I'm all up and through your game room; I see ya."

Ty giggled. "I guess you're inspector gadget. I needed to come visit my mom, so it was only right that I kill two birds with one stone. While we're on that subject, I should go ahead and tell you that me and Nasir are together. I put this thang on him and now he can't leave me alone. We've been rocking tight for almost two weeks now, so you know it's real."

"Didn't I tell you before he can't be your man if he belongs to someone else? It's ok to fuck him every now and then; but you done took it to a whole other level. The funny part is that you actually believe what's coming out of your mouth." Khia said with sarcasm.

"You and Paige blow me with how y'all feel about my situation. Again, it's my situation, so let me deal with it how I may. At the end of the day, when it's all said and done, the chips will land wherever they choose to. Now, I know when you come back to Atlanta with *us* you're going to have to figure out exactly what you're going to be doing there."

"I won't comment on all of what you said; just know I will be signing up for G.E.D. classes. I really do need to get my shit together. The first of every month I will have to travel back to Miami so that I can make sure everything is still straight here. Are you cool with paying for my flight once a month?"

"I'm so glad you're down for it, consider it done. I gotcha girl. I want the best for you, like I know you would want for me if I was in your situation."

"We gotta have each other's back cause if we don't, who will?" As the words rolled off of her tongue, Khia got an instant pain in her stomach. She repeated to herself: *remember I'm doing this because I didn't have any other choice.* She was still trying to justify what she was about to do to someone who'd been a friend and more than family to her.

Chapter Twelve

Back To Our
Regular Scheduled Programs

"Baby, I think it's time we have a sit down talk—just you and me. The way things have been going lately isn't like us. Going two weeks without so much as a good morning, good night or an I love you isn't right. That's not how people in love act. I'm back now baby and my complete focus is on getting us right. Can you miss out on this one meeting—not just for me, but for us?" she asked with pleading eyes.

Nasir stopped in his tracks to listen to what his wife had to say. He was getting ready to head out and meet Ty for a private dinner he had set up in a romantic setting. He was now debating whether he should skip out on the dinner with her and tend to his wife, seeing as though since he met Ty he'd been neglecting his wife in more ways than one; emotionally, physically, mentally and intellectually. He didn't know how Tyquasia would take him standing her up, but it was time he made things ok with his wife.

"You know what? I really didn't feel like going to that meeting anyway. The club owners will be in town for a couple of days, so hopefully we can reschedule it; if not, you just cost me fifty thousand dollars so you're gonna have to make up for that." he joked.

"Awh, thank you baby. I'm happy that you're willing to stay home and work on us; that shows me that this marriage means something to you. First things first, our communication is way off. That's one of our biggest problems. I want you to be able to come to me and tell me when you're not happy or not pleased with something I'm doing. Let's address the problem right then instead of letting a little problem grow and manifest into something greater."

In his usual calm and chill demeanor, Nasir pulled Lorraine next to him and kissed her forehead gently. "You know that I love you and that I would do anything under the sun to make sure that you're happy. Why don't I feel like I get the same in return? Before you say it, I'm not just talking about sexually, although that is a big part of the problem. I mean shit…I'm not anywhere near dead over here. I'm twenty-six years old. We have to come to a compromise on that 'cause I got some shit that I wanna do to you, I just want you to be willing to let me do it. I already know you're going to enjoy it if you just gave some of my advances half a chance."

"We can do that. I'll say this, I'm willing to try anything once; who knows I may like it."

"We can get started right now." He said as he slid the strap of her tank dress off of her shoulder leaving a kiss on her exposed skin. "Stand up," he instructed.

Lorraine did as she was told. Nasir slipped the other strap off and let the dress fall to the floor. "I want you right here on every part of this sectional sofa."

"Right here?" Lorraine asked apprehensive, but excited at the same time.

Instead of replying, he guided her to the back of the couch and just like in the dream that he had about Tyquasia, he placed Lorraine's leg up on the back of the couch, unbuckled his pants and let them drop to the floor. He pulled his boxer briefs down and without warning he inserted himself.

Lorraine wasn't used to the things that Nasir was doing to her. She was used to him taking his time with her, basically guiding her or preparing her for everything he did to her. Not this time though. This time Nasir was in full control; calling all of the shots.

Lorraine was once again battling herself to stay in the moment. She didn't know why she would shut down during sex between them; but often times she did. It wasn't that he didn't know what he was doing, because he put it down. There was something standing in the way of her fully enjoying the dick lashin' he was putting on her.

Lorraine moaned and yelled out Nasir's name as they switched positions. Even though her erotic noises were made up, she tried to make them sound as real as possible. Nasir on the other hand had his eyes closed the entire time. He was imaging that he was really banging Ty's back out and that she was the one calling his name. He put in extra work; working her over time as if this were their last time. As they lay on the thick, plush Italian throw rug in yet another position, while he slow stroked her from the side, Lorraine commented, "Damn baby! You ain't never fucked me like this before. Seems like somebody missed me cause you're going in," Lorraine said out loud as she inwardly thought, *it's almost as if he's fucking me like I'm someone else.* The thought came through just as clear as day and night. At that very moment Nasir came long and hard. Lorraine lay there stiff as a board. Her body full of tension, but Nasir was too far gone in his own world to even notice it.

Chapter Thirteen

He Ain't Nothing But A Dog

Tyquasia stormed in her apartment pissed. She kicked her heels off at the door.

"What the fuck is all that noise?" Khia yelled running down the stairs.

"It's me bitch. Nasir got me all types of fucked up! Remember when I told you that I was going to meet him at the hotel tonight? Well, when I got there the woman at the front desk instructed me to take the elevator to the rooftop, so I did. When I walked through the exit door it was like something out of a romantic movie scene the way things were set up. There were candles, rose petals, a table in the middle of the rooftop with two chairs; very intimate like. So I walked over to the table expecting Nasir to come out of the shadows at any second. I sat down at the table after about fifteen minutes. I felt like something was up so I sent him a text letting him know that I made it to the hotel, loved my surprise and I was waiting on him. Thirty minutes went by—no Nasir—no reply.

I lifted the lid off of one of the plates and saw that it was fire-seared steak topped with sautéed shrimp with a side of buttered asparagus and garlic mash potatoes. I ate a sautéed shrimp, grabbed my shit, and left mad as hell. The woman at the front desk who had instructed me to go to the roof saw the angry, hurt, look on my face and asked me did I not like my surprise. I had to literally stop myself from snapping on her. I simply replied with gritted teeth that it was a great surprise that was supposed to involve two people. I looked around and then turned back to her and asked, "Now, I don't see the other person; do you?" She stood there stuck. I asked her, 'What? Cat got your tongue?' After that I walked off because she wasn't the one I should've been taking my anger out on. I have been blowing up Nasir's phone ever since then. Do you think I got an answer? Hell fuckin' no! Ugh!"

"Damn! He did all that for you and then turned around and stood you up? Something must've prevented him from being there tonight. I saw how y'all interacted in Miami. I know he would've been there if he could've," Khia sympathized.

"I know he would've replied to my text or answered one of my fifteen missed calls that went to his phone; but he didn't. That's the bottom line. Now I'm starting to think if I really know this dude like I think I do? I've been so caught up in sex, trying to figure out what's happening with us and what he's going to do about his wife, that I don't think I've truly gotten to know him as a person," Ty said. She plopped down on the couch.

"Listen, you're a smart girl Ty. You'll figure it out. Read between the lines; he's a married man who set up a fabulous dinner for the two of you, but didn't show up to it and didn't answer any of your calls when you were trying to find out why he wasn't there. It's obvious that his wife did something to make him stay home. I've dealt with enough married men to know that when things like this happen, it's either one of two things going on; one, the kids got sick and he decided to stay home with them, but since we know he doesn't have any kids that's out, or two, his wife had a feeling that he was up to no good so she threw a guilt trip on him which led him to stay home. If the second option is the case, then they would have less than enjoyable sex while the husband reminisces about his side pussy, or in your case, his mistress," Khia said as she zoned out.

"I was thinking something like that probably happened; it's cool though. Fuck him! I'm not about to even sweat it. Now Miss Thang where are you going in that get up? Mind you all of the items that you have on look like they came from my closet. Damn! Do you have on my thongs too?"

"Oh, you noticed." Khia laughed. "Well, I went and did a little shopping in your massive closet. I hope you don't mind. Half of the stuff in there still had price tags on it. I'm going on a dinner date with an instructor that I met while I was signing up for my GED classes. Since you're back, can I hold your car to meet him? I don't want him knowing where I'm staying just yet."

"I don't mind this time, but keep your ass out of my closet. You say you have a date with an instructor huh? Sounds like the right kind of dude for you. He's not married is he?" Ty questioned.

"No, he's not married. I'm done with married men. Hopefully after your experience with one, you'll be done too. I've had enough for one lifetime. From the talk I had with him earlier, I gathered that he's a cool, legit dude; and I wouldn't mind getting to know him a little more." *Damn with all the questions! Just give me the keys so I can be out of this muthafucka,* Khia thought.

"That's just what I wanted to hear. Take care of my baby; hoe, 'cause I will bust yo' ass if anything happens to my car."

Ty handed Khia the keys.

"I'm going to take care of your car; I know it's your heart. Are those the new Jessica Simpson shoes you brought while we were in Miami thrown by the door?"

"Yep, that's them. I don't care about nothing right now."

"Good, so you won't care if I rock them with this outfit?"

Ty looked over what Khia had on, which was a turquoise sleeveless peplum top that was one size too small, and a red pencil skirt. The two color contrast really worked. Then she thought about the lavender Jessica Simpson pumps she'd just kicked off by the door and she wondered why Khia would want to do that.

"Suit yourself…sure, go ahead."

"Thanks girl. See you later on tonight or maybe in the morning depending on how well this date goes," Khia said with a wink. Cheer up. Eat some chocolate and watch *Player's Club*, *Set It Off* or *Two Can Play That Game*. Hint, hint. Khia winked as she walked out the door.

* * * * *

Khia really didn't have a date, but she did plan on going to the club to grind up on a few eligible bachelors. Hell, wasn't anything wrong with that; Benzino wasn't home yet. First things first, she had to accomplish her mission. See what Tyquasia didn't know was that Khia paid very close attention to everything Ty did; so every time they were out together and getting ready to head home, Ty would always enter an address into her GPS, put the automated voice on silent, and follow the directions past a very prestigious neighborhood and then act as if she'd gotten lost or taken a wrong turn. Khia figured out that, her need to redirect her movements must have been due to her being in Nasir's neighborhood. Now it was her job to find out exactly what estate he lived in, the entry and exit points, what kind of cars he and his wife drove and any other things she could get while snooping around.

She drove up to the end of the Cruz's driveway with the lights out. She put on an all black trench coat so that she wouldn't be noticed. She slid out of the car and tip toed up the roundabout drive way. There were three cars sitting in a row. Khia pulled out her cell phone and stored the type of cars, colors and license plate numbers on each one of them.

Damn, maybe it wasn't such a good idea to wear these five-inch heels and this tight ass skirt. Khia managed as best she could; getting more details around the property and then she tiptoed back to the car, and just as quietly as she came, she left. She was trying to get as much information as she could before she would have to go back to Miami and visit Benzino. She thought the more information she had, the quicker she would have to stop the whole spy operation.

"Now that that's done, I can head to the club and turn that bitch out." *The bitches are going to be hating tonight 'cause I'll be the prettiest chick up in there.*

* * * * *

"Professor Stanley is giving us the business. It's like we can't catch a break. Quiz...tests, exams...that's all I hear when we're in his class."

"I know girl! But at least you've caught back up on most of your work. I'm glad you're focused again. Oh, shit! Looks like I spoke too soon. Here comes 'Mr. Full of Excuses.'" Paige taunted when she saw Nasir walking toward them in the distance.

"I'm not ready to see or talk to him just yet. That nigga hurt me and I don't do 'hurt' well," Ty sulked.

"No, it's time. You need to face him. Be strong. Hear what he has to say; but most importantly, don't give in" Paige said coaching her.

"Listen, I know it's been a couple of weeks since you've seen or heard from me, but my wife has been in my ass constantly. Can you just stop and talk to me, damn!" Nasir said as he followed behind Ty.

"What! Tell me what it is that you have to say to me that's so important that you gotta blow my phone up all morning? If I'm not mistaken, there was a night, not too long ago, when I called you fifteen times and texted you and I never got a simple answer or reply," Ty said fuming.

"Tyquasia, you need to understand where I'm coming from. You know how things were before you got involved with me. I'm married, shit came up that night and I couldn't get to you." Nasir's eyes pleaded for Ty to forgive him.

Paige sucked her teeth. "Come on Ty, you don't have to sit up here and listen to this bullshit. You don't have to settle for what he's telling you either. Remember what I told you, you're too bad to continue playing second best."

"Listen chick, I know you're tryna be here for your friend, but this really ain't got nothing to do with you," Nasir said matter-of-factly.

"Paige, can you give us a second. I'm going to hear him out and then we can keep it moving." Paige gave Ty a look as if to ask her if she was sure that's how she wanted to handle the situation. Ty replied, "I'm good, I got this." Paige took one last look at Nasir and walked a few feet away.

"It's good to see that your friends ride for you like you ride for them. She means business, doesn't she?" he joked.

Tyquasia stood there showing no emotion. She was unfazed by his attempt to break the ice between them.

"I know I was wrong for not texting or calling you for the last couple of weeks. I'm sorry for that. I need you to give me some slack because you know what my situation is. There wasn't one day that went by that you weren't constantly on my mind. I love you Ty and I want you to be a part of my life. I don't want you to shut me out. I know I have to do something about my current status and I will—the time is near."

Tyquasia studied his face as he said every word. "You love me huh? And you came to this realization because we haven't been in contact in a few weeks?" Ty asked.

Nasir caressed the side of her face. "You're so gorgeous; you know that right? To be honest with you, I realized that I loved you the day before I set up that surprise on the rooftop. I had things all planned out. I was going to tell you how I felt about you then. Let's pick up where we left off."

Even though Nasir had hurt her by disappearing on her, Ty still had feelings for him and a strong connection to him. She knew she still wanted him to be in her life too. She was missing his touch, his smile and his smell. "I will give you another chance, but I want you to promise me that nothing like this will ever happen again and that soon, and very soon, you will tell your wife it's over between you two because you've found someone that really makes you happy. If you can't promise me that…this talk is in vain."

"I can promise you that I'm going to take care of my business so that shit like this won't happen again. Soon you won't have to worry about Lorraine. I want us to get together tomorrow. She'll be flying out of town for a gig, so I'll be all yours. I will text you with the name of the hotel where we will be staying without any interruptions."

"No, Nasir I'm not doing the hotel thing; I'm passed that. I wanna come stay at your house. Is that a problem?" Ty asked with her eye brow raised.

"My house? Nawh, that's not a problem. We can chill out there for a few." He looked at his watch for the second time during their conversation.

"Do you have some where that you need to be right now?" Ty asked with an attitude.

"Yeah, I need to get over to my office. I have some meetings set up, but I couldn't go another day without seeing or hearing from you."

"Ok, well text me later then."

"I will," he said. He got close to her ear and whispered, "You look edible in this outfit, but I'd rather see you with nothing but ya heels on. Damn…big man and I have really missed you. Be ready for us tomorrow." He hugged her tightly and kissed her lovingly which made her weak in the knees.

As soon as Nasir walked off Paige ran up. "I thought your ass was going to be strong, stand your ground and most of all stick it to his ass. You were going strong in the beginning, then what happened? Now y'all back at it again huh? I bet he sold you a bunch of dreams and fake promises that he's not going to live up to," Paige said going in.

"Like I told you, 'I got this' is all you need to know. You don't play Tyquasia Roberts for second fiddle. I got something in store for him and until it happens, I'm going to play my role. Now fuck talking about him; what are the plans for tonight?"

"That's my girl! We can hit up a dorm party and get shit faced."

"I forget sometimes that you're white." Ty laughed. "Getting shit faced it is, but I'm not staying out all night; like I said, I have a role to play and it starts tomorrow."

"I will have you back to your apartment with enough time for you to rest up and as you say, "play your role." Just call me when you get done getting dressed and I'll swing by and pick you up so you won't have to drive."

"Ok, that's a bet! See you later."

* * * * *

Ty dug through her earring box looking for her other Chanel earring that went perfectly with her Chanel bandage dress. *Maybe Khia has seen it,* she thought.

She went to Khia's room and knocked on the door. She heard what sounded like someone whispering, but she figured it was the TV. Khia opened the door with her cell phone in hand. "Girl, you scared me. I was in here watching *Friday The 13th*, the original one. What's up?"

"Yeah, I kinda figured that you were watching TV since I heard voices. I wanted to know if you'd seen my other Chanel earring. Paige is going to be here any minute and I can't find it."

"Nope. I haven't seen it, but I did wanna ask you if I could use your Japanese Cherry Blossom body wash and lotion? I'm trying to get my sip on, while I relax in a nice aroma therapy bath so that I'll be relaxed for my flight."

"Yeah, you can use it, but how in the hell do you know what's in my bathroom when you have your own bathroom to use? You know what…don't answer that, we'll talk about it later. After you get the body wash and lotion, keep ya ass out of my bathroom! Do me a favor and get the door; I'm sure that's Paige. Tell her I'm coming.

I don't want to be around that bitch, Khia thought. She answered the door. "Ugh, it's you. Ty said she'll be down in a minute. I guess you can come in." Khia said. She left the door open and turned around and headed to the kitchen. She grabbed a glass, a bottle of wine and a cork screw.

This little hood rat ain't got no fuckin' manners, Paige thought as she came in and closed the door herself. Khia walked back past Paige and shot her a nasty look as she continued up the stairs with her hands full.

While Paige sat and waited for Ty, she heard a phone vibrating on the island top in the kitchen. She picked up the phone thinking it was Ty's phone. She saw that the caller was from an unknown name and unknown number. She recalled Ty telling her that Benzino's calls always come through like that. Paige was curious to hear what the infamous Benzino sounded like so she answered the phone. The automated voice came on, "You have a call from "Khia, this is Benz, answer!" an inmate in the..."

"Oh shit," Paige said as she fumbled with the phone. When she heard the deep voice say, "Khia this is Benz," she hung up. That's when she saw the front screen with the display name running across the top which said, *Khia The Queen Of The South* and had Khia's picture as the wallpaper.

Damn! This is her phone. What the fuck is Ty's ex doing calling Khia's phone. Mmm hmm, a nasty low down dirty bitch! I gotta tell Ty about this shit right after we get our party on. I know her ass ain't gonna want to go if I tell her this shit now. Ain't that 'bout a bitch!

Paige put the phone down exactly how she found it and walked back to the couch just in time to see Ty coming down the stairs.

"Hey chick, you look cute. Sorry it took so long, I was looking for my earring and couldn't find it so I decided to go with these. How do they look with this dress?" Ty asked striking a pose.

"The earrings are nice, they're not too much and not too plain. It's the dress that's going to get all of the attention though."

"Oh this?" Ty said doing a mini spin. "It's a Chanel bandage dress I pulled out of my closet. It still had the tags on it. Anyway, let's get going. If this party ain't poppin' we can hit up a club. I'm in a partying mood tonight."

Chapter Fourteen

An Eye Opener

"Girl, I love coming to the club with you. You always know how to have a good time," Paige said giggling from her tipsiness. She wasn't much of a drinker, so after two cups of *Jamaican Me Wet*, she was saucy.

"What can I say, I love to go out and enjoy myself; especially after being in a relationship for three years with a man that prevented me from going anywhere. Hell yeah, after that experience of course I'm gonna want to get out and party every chance I get." Ty replied giggling as if she'd said something funny.

"Speaking of Benzino, have you talked to him since you've moved up here?"

"Why do I feel like you're beating around the bush? When I first moved here he was calling my phone a lot a few times a day; but in the last few weeks I haven't heard anything from him. I was thinking maybe his phone privileges were taken from him or maybe he just got the hint that I'm not fucking with his ass anymore. Either way, I'm happy he's not calling anymore."

"What would you say if I told you neither one of those reasons are right?"

Ty looked at Paige with a confused expression on her face. "I would ask you how the fuck would you know?"

"Let's just say everyone you have around you ain't to be trusted. Ya girl Khia has been talking to him—probably feeding him information on your whereabouts and how you're living. This is just my assumption, but I can guarantee you any amount of money that I'm not too far off from the truth."

"So now you're going to throw salt on her name—telling me how I shouldn't trust her and all this other shit; right? I mean, what is it with you chicks? I know, I know...I'm just one person, but there's enough of me to go around. I can be a friend to both of you with no problem. Benzino doesn't like Khia; never has. He hated when I used to hang around her or even talk to her on the phone so that can't be the case."

"Yes, you're a great friend, but don't flatter yourself. What I'm telling you are real facts, and now that you said he doesn't like her at all, it makes me more sure about what I think is going on." Paige proceeded to run down the story of what happened while she was at Ty's place waiting on her to get ready. The look on Tyquasia's face changed from shocked to anger.

"So, what I'm telling you is that the whole time I was thinking it was your phone until I heard him say, "Khia this Benz," and then as soon as I hung up, that's when I saw her wall paper and the name on her screen, *Khia The Queen of The South* scrolling across the top. Trust me, I was as shocked as you are right now, but I knew I couldn't tell you right then because I knew that one: you wasn't gonna want to go out anymore, and two: you probably would've killed the bitch."

"Damn Paige, you should've told me when I came

downstairs, regardless of what you thought was or wasn't going to happen. Now I gotta deal with this conniving, two-faced ass bitch! I know you're not lying because how else would you know about Khia's phone. Just drive faster. I hope I can catch her ass before she leaves my place."

Paige did as she was told and put the pedal to the metal. When they got back to Tyquasia's apartment they jumped out and ran inside. Ty went to the kitchen and grabbed a knife. "I'm gonna kill that bitch if she's still here."

Ty took the steps two at a time with Paige right on her trail. Without knocking, she busted in the room to find the bed made up. "Damn, what times is it? Her flight probably already left. I need to know what her slick ass has been up to and what she has told Benz so far. Fuck it, I've got something for her. I know just the person to handle this." She ran back downstairs, grabbed her phone out of her purse and called D.

"Damn baby, what's up? It's been a minute since I've heard from you. I was almost ready to catch a plane down there to make sure everything is Gucci," D said in a thick, up North accent.

"D, I need you to take care of a situation for me. It seems that there's been a snake slithering around me this whole time. Khia has been talking to Benzino; for how long I don't know, but I just found this out a few minutes ago."

"Word? Say no more. Is she still in Atlanta with you?"

"No, she just got a flight back to Miami."

"Aiight. Let me pack my shit. I'll be headed to Miami later on today. I had something else planned, but this shit needs to be taken care of first. When am I going to get to see you again? I miss ya. I know there are a lot of things going on in our lives, but you said it wouldn't fuck with us; looks to me like it's fucking with us."

"I can't talk about that right now. Just go ahead and handle that situation. I don't know what Khia has going on, but I can't let it fuck up our plans. We'll figure the rest out later."

"Yeah, alright; consider it handled. I'll hit you up when I'm back in my city." D said with a bit of aggression. Ty hung up because she knew that it wasn't the right time or place to have the conversation that D wanted to have.

"What is D going to do to Khia?" Paige said, wondering who D was.

"Oh, now you're worried about Khia? D is just going to teach her a lesson. You can't play both sides of the field; you're either with me or against me and she knew that." Ty said angrily pacing the floor.

"Trust, I'm not worried about her; I was just wondering. From the sounds of it, D don't play. I would hate to be Khia right now."

"Yeah, if you're going to be my friend, all I ask is that you always keep it real with me. And tell me shit on time from now on!"

"You got it! As soon as some shit happens, you'll be the first to know."

Chapter Fifteen

Checkmate

Khia was ready to get her visit with Benzino over with. Although she was happy to see him, she was really ready to be done with the whole spying deal. Ty was her girl, and at the end of the day, she didn't want to have Tyquasia's blood on her hands. When Benzino walked through the door she thought he would be a little happier to see her. Especially since she had information for him, but instead he had a unit on his face and his demeanor showed that he wasn't happy.

"Go ahead and tell me what you got for me," Benz said as he sat down.

Khia pulled out a piece of folded paper and held it up as she unfolded it to show that it was nothing more than a piece of paper. Benzino took the paper, folded it back up and placed it in his pocket. "Let me drop some shit on you. The next time that bitch Ty knocks on the door while you're on the phone with me, you tell me to hold on; don't just hang up in my face. And what's up when I called yo' mu'fuckin' phone back, you didn't answer? Do that shit again and see what I do to you when I get out of here!" Benzino seethed.

"Wait, I didn't get a call from you after I hung up with you. I went to answer the door for Tyquasia's friend Paige and then I went to the kitchen to get a bottle of wine, a glass and cork screw. I had to sit my phone down on the island in the kitchen while I looked for the items. When I had everything I needed I headed back. . ." Her words trailed off as she recalled the scene. "Paige had to have answered my phone because when I picked my phone up to call the cab I didn't have a missed call; so I didn't even know that you called. Shit, did you say your name on the recording?"

"Yeah, I said my name. I always say my fuckin' name when I call."

"I told you before that you didn't have to do that. I always know who it is when you call." Khia whispered under her breath.

"What did you say? Speak up when you're talking! You mean to tell me you done slipped up and allowed some bird brain named Paige to have access to your phone?" Benz snapped sitting up from his crouched position.

"She wasn't supposed to be snooping around while she was waiting on Ty to finish getting dressed. If I would've caught her going through my phone, I would've beaten the white off of her ass like I should've done the first time we got into."

"Check me out…I don't know what's going on here, but you better get to the bottom of it and get there real fast. Ain't no telling what tricks Ty has up her sleeve now. Something's going on 'cause niggas that used to fuck with me and be on my team when I was out in them streets ain't been fuckin' with me. They ain't taking my calls, coming for visits, or even checked to see if a nigga needed something or anything else. Those niggas think I'm done for, but when I get back on my feet in them streets I'm gone have something for all of them. I'll be getting out of here any day now on the strength that the jail systems in Florida are too crowded, my crime was non-violent and I got time for good behavior. I need you to get your ass back to Atlanta on the next plane flying out. You're dismissed."

"Why do I have to go back there? I got you all of the information that you need."

"Bitch, don't question me; just do as I say. Bye!"

"Khia sat and stared at him for a minute longer than she needed to. Looking into his eyes she saw the real person inside and for the first time she regretted doing what she'd been doing. She wished she could take it all back, but she couldn't. She'd laid down with the devil now it was time to face all of the consequences. She knew if she said another word that Benzino would probably flip out, so she got up and left.

The bus ride from the jail was a short one, but the walk from the closet bus stop to the projects felt like it was taking forever. She was half way to her apartment when the string on her stiletto came loose, she stopped mid-stride to wrap it back up her leg and tie it. *For these heels to be so cute, they're always coming loose. I bet the real Gucci heels don't do this, damn knock offs! I'm gonna have Benz buy me some real ones.*

While Khia was fussing with the strap on her heels, a smoked-out, black-on-black Audi R8 pulled up on the side of her. The person exited the car and walked up to her and put the barrel of a Kel-Tec PF9 .9mm pistol to her dome. Khia jumped and started crying immediately. "Please sir, I don't live in the projects and I don't have any money. If you let me go, when my boyfriend Benzino gets out I'll make sure he hits you off with whatever you want; just please don't hurt me." she whimpered.

"I told Ty that bitches can't be trusted. Y'all just ain't loyal, that's why you gotta keep ya kind out they business."

At the mention of Tyquasia's name, Khia looked up and instantly knew who the gun totting' bandit was. "D, why are you out here holding a fuckin' gun to my head like you done lost your fuckin' mind?" Khia yelled, no longer afraid.

"Hoe, watch yo' fuckin' mouth. Don't say my name like you know me and I ain't never personally fucked with you on that level. Benzino is ya man's right?" D bellowed.

"No, he's not my man. I thought by saying his name whoever was robbing me would back down cause Benzino has pull out here in these streets. You know that's Ty's man. I never told anyone what I knew about you and Ty..." Her words were caught in her throat as D punched her, causing a sharp pain to shoot through her body while her eye swelled up.

"Don't speak about what the fuck me and her got going on." D gripped the chrome framed, navy blue grip of the gun with intense pressure.

"I have wasted enough time with you. I was originally sent here to fuck yo' hoe ass up, but now that I'm here looking at you face to face, I've decided to send a message to your little *boyfriend*. That was my pussy he was diggin' in every night for three years. Ty ain't fucked up with that nigga no more, so if he comes fuckin' with her off some information you done told him, he'll get the same treatment as you." With that said, D pulled back the hammer and let the double pump action gun's bullets shatter Khia's skull; droppin' her on impact. Brain matter and blood began to cover the sidewalk and seep into the cracks on the pavement.

D smoothly walked back over to the car and rode off. D sent Ty a text letting her know that the issue was taken care of....Permanently!

Chapter Sixteen

I Only See One Ending In Sight

When Ty got the text informing her that Khia would no longer be a problem, she was happy until she saw the word, "permanently." Yes, she was mad that Khia had betrayed her trust. And yes, she had said some things like, "*I'm going to kill that bitch if she's still here*" when she found out that Khia was talking to Benz and being a snake behind her back. But she wasn't happy hearing the word, "permanently." She knew what D was capable of, so she also had to know what she was getting herself into when she called D to teach Khia a lesson. *It is what it is now,* she thought. She couldn't bring Khia back and tell her not to be affiliated with Benz or even tell her to be loyal like a friend should be. What was done was done.

Ty thought about her situation while she drove over to Nasir's place. Today would be the day that she would give him an ultimatum. She walked up to the front door and walked in without ringing the doorbell or knocking—like it was her place and she could just do that if she wanted to.

"Well hey there sexy. I didn't hear you knock or ring the doorbell. I'm glad you're here." Nasir said giving her a peck on the lips. "You know you got a nigga sprung if he gets in the kitchen and cooks for you." he winked. "Let me take your bag for you."

Ty handed him her overnight bag. "Is that so? What are you cooking for me?"

"My specialty. You know I'm more of a healthy eater, so I made us some homemade spicy Italian turkey sausage and spinach lasagna."

"Mmm, that sounds good. Got my stomach talking to me. You look very provoking with that apron and those sweat pants on. I can see your dick print." Ty said admiring his physique. *Stay focused, I gotta get an understanding tonight,* Ty coached herself to get back on the right track.

"I'll be serving you tonight, so just sit down and relax."

Ty did as she was told. She made her way to the dining room. She sat and watched Nasir move around the kitchen. *A man who cooks, how sexy is that?*

Once everything was ready, Nasir brought it over to the table and served Ty.

"I think it's the sweetest thing that you're cooking and serving me and all I have to do is sit back and relax. I love it because this isn't something I'm used to. I'm usually the one in the kitchen putting in that work." Ty said sipping some wine.

"If we were married, I would make sure you get this type of treatment all of the time. You deserve nothing but the best."

"Speaking of "if we were married" that's never going to happen if you continue to be married. Like you said, I deserve the best; which means I don't deserve this situation I'm in with you. What can we do to make this right?" Ty asked eyeing him intensely.

"On some real shit, I've had the divorce talk with Lorr... with her. From what I gather, she's not having it. I think her exact words were, 'If anyone wants out of this marriage they'll go out by body bag only.'" Nasir said, stretching the truth to see how Ty would react.

"By body bag hmm? I'm starting to feel like that can be arranged. I hate a pest of a woman. When a man is done with you, leave. Shit, there's other pipes out there in the world; and vice versa, when a woman is done with a man they should leave."

"What do you mean you're starting to think that can be arranged?" he asked taking her hand into his.

"Just what I said. I've never done anything violent or vicious to anyone besides a fight I got into in elementary school; but I don't mind getting my hands dirty if I have to."

Nasir raised his eyebrow and cleared his throat. "How would you do it, you know…if you were to do it?"

"I would probably give her two shots to the heart or I could slice her neck with one swipe of the blade. Nawh that's too messy." Ty joked. "I don't know, however I do it, I would take care of my business and make sure there aren't any witnesses around when I did."

Nasir went in for the kill. "That's the only way I see us being together without any outside interruptions or drama. Will you do it?"

Ty sat there thinking about the conversation they were having. She was no killer, even though she'd seen it done in movies and around her way when she lived in Miami. "Yes, I think I can do it; no…I know I can do it for *us*."

Nasir pushed his chair back, stood up and walked over to Ty, picking her up from her seat. She wrapped her legs around his waist and asked, "What are you doing? We're not even done eating."

"You're it, you're the one for me—my everything—and

I have an appetite for something else." He said, kissing her chest over and over again. Nasir carried Ty upstairs past two doors to a room that had, "*The White Room*" carved in cursive on the door.

"Is this the bedroom that you share with her?"

"Yeah, this is one of our bedrooms. We also have a black room that has the other half of our things in it. She couldn't decide which room she liked better since they're both master bedrooms."

Ty got hot all of a sudden as if she was turned on by the fact that she was about to fuck him in the bed that he shared with his wife. 'Well, we need to make it to the black room after we get done breaking in the white room." Ty replied.

"Shit, I'm down for that," he said struggling to turn on the lights. When he got the lights on, Ty saw why the room was called the white room, it was decorated in all white and the lighting was black lights so the room lit up with a florescent glow of purple.

"Oh shit, this is something different. A black light in the bedroom is hot!"

"I thought you would say that."

Nasir kissed Ty with a lot of intensity and then he laid her down on the bed. He held her leg up and removed the heel that elongated her left leg. He then proceeded to place one soft manicured toe in his mouth at a time. He took his time as he sucked her toes. He removed the second heel and did the same thing. Low moans escaped from Ty's mouth. He'd found a spot that Ty didn't even know was there. She got wet; wetter than she'd ever been from a touch or from someone sucking her neck which she thought was her only spot.

Nasir licked and kissed his way up her legs until he got

to her thighs where the hemline of her dress rested. He rubbed his hands slowly, going further under her dress and teasing her by swiping his finger across her panties and her smooth pussy. He always knew how to get her to the peak of no return. She was yearning for him in every way possible. Nasir finally stopped teasing her and tasted her sweet juice box. It was as if it tasted better every time he went back for more. She started to scoot back on the bed while Nasir gave her a tongue lashing. He wasn't going to let up.

"Uh uh, where are you going? Bring that ass back here." He said in a low tone and then wrapped his well-defined arms around her thighs, pulling her back to him as he continued his quest with a vice grip on her thighs. She wasn't getting away this time. He wanted her to enjoy every flick of his tongue. Her thighs locked around his head, squeezing it as she climaxed violently, squirting her juices right into his mouth. Nasir was just getting started he was about to dick whip her into a coma.

Chapter Seventeen

A Friend Is All I Need

Lorraine usually didn't take a gig after she'd been working for two weeks straight out of town; but getting away from Atlanta and Nasir was needed. A breather was what she was thinking when she got the call from Nancy about a gig that needed to be approved. It was an interview and photo shoot with Philly Trend Magazine. The interview was going great until the questions started to get more and more personal about her home life and her marriage to Nasir Cruz.

"My next question gets a little more personal, but that's what the people of Philadelphia want. They want to know more about Lorraine the person. Since your last visit a couple of weeks ago, the buzz behind it has been crazy around here. Do you and Nasir have any plans on having kids anytime soon?"

"That's good to hear. I love Philadelphia, they show me a lot of love every time I come here. Nasir and I have had the children talk a few times, but right now, neither of our careers permit us to have kids. When I...I mean, 'we' have a child, I want us to be able to give our child our full attention and also provide a great life and future for them. The only way I see us doing that is to continue working at the pace we are now and then kick back and relax later."

"Ok, that's understandable. How does your husband feel about how much you work? You have to be one of the hardest working women in the modeling industry. Every time I see you in a magazine, you're at an event in a different state. Most men will say that a woman's place is at home and in the kitchen. You challenge that. I know that's right, get it while you can." Tracy the co-owner of Philly Trend Magazine said.

Is this chick trying to come for me? "Yes, I am a hard working woman just trying to make a name and brand for myself. As I stated before, my husband understands that I hope, but if he was a man that didn't understand, guess what…I would leave him in a heartbeat. So baby, if you're reading this interview—know that. Make sure you quote me on that Tracy."

"Well said, and you're quoted on everything that you say. I'm all for independent sistahs doing their own thang. I feel so comfortable interviewing you. I think that's because you keep it real. With that being said, I just thought of my next question. With all of the traveling you and your husband do, y'all rarely get time to spend together. With Nasir hosting and promoting a hot party every week or every other week, you're not concerned about him cheating on you with one of those beautiful women from a party? I read the blog sites, papers and magazines—hell my magazine is one—and I know he's been in them a few times for speculations, but no real evidence."

Lorraine was feeling uncomfortable and ready to get in defense mode to shut down whatever speculations Tracy was trying to put out there. She looked over to Nancy and gave her the "end the interview now" look.

I know this woman is trying to get me to act a fool up in here. "Let me go ahead and put this out there for all to read and know that this came straight from the horse's mouth when reading it. My husband is just that, *my husband.* He's not going anywhere. Yes, he travels and so do I. He does parties most of the time and he's around scantily dressed women, but that doesn't bother me because I'm secure within me. That's where a lot of women go wrong. You need to be secure with yourself before you can be secure with anyone else. All those speculations are false and to all of the people claiming differently—show some proof. Where's the proof? That's right, there isn't any. Everybody wants Nasir Cruz, but can't nobody have him because I have him. He's mine; period, point blank!"

"Well, I guess Mrs. Cruz cleared that up and you're reading it here first. On that note, we're going to end the interview here. You can find her on all social media sites under Lorraine Cruz. Thank you for taking the time to interview with me and answer all of my questions."

After changing into four different looks, the shoot was finally over. Lorraine couldn't get out of there fast enough.

"This shit is unbelievable. I need to talk to Nasir and tell him about the shit that went on during that interview. I know he's probably not going to read the interview, but I know like hell he's going to hear about it. I didn't mean to spazz out like that, but she took me there." Lorraine said to Nancy as they walked out. Her mind continued to chastise her, *I exaggerated the hell out of my truth too. I don't even want to be around Nasir right now, but I did the right thing; I had to save face in there.*

"She made me a little hot as well. Especially the way

she asked that last question as if she already had her mind made up that Nasir was running around cheating with every woman he meets. Don't let that bother you though. It won't be your first interview to go like that and I'm sure it won't be your last." Nancy replied checking emails on her Blackberry.

"I really just wanna take a day to myself. I have another business venture that I'm going to get into so I'm going to stay in Philly for maybe a day or two more. You can go ahead and head back tonight as planned."

"Business venture? Isn't that something your manager and publicist should know about? I'm cool with you staying a day longer because you don't have anything scheduled for tomorrow, but I need you back in Atlanta first thing Friday morning. Remember you have an appearance at 3:00 P.M."

"When my new business venture is thoroughly discussed you will know about it. Trust me, I'm not getting into anything without involving you. You've been rocking with me from the start. I will be sure to get back to Atlanta on time for my appearance. You know how much I hate being late to any event."

"As long as you know I got your back. I'm going to get a few things together in my room and then I'm heading out. I'll see you Friday morning back in ATL. Call me if you need anything or email me, you may hear from me faster that way." Nancy said joking.

"Ok, you can count on it." Lorraine said walking in the direction of her room.

A nice hot bath in the whirlpool tub was the first thing that popped into her mind when she got settled back in her room. She ran some water and added her favorite body wash and bath salts. She wanted to soak for a little while and think through her current dilemma. She dipped into the steamy hot water full of bubbles, careful not to splash any water because she had her phone in her hand checking emails, updating her Facebook and replying to tweets.

She was about to log out when she noticed that she had a tweet from DomtheKing. The tweet said *@ModelLC No email miss lady ;)*

Lorraine instantly knew who the tweet was from. A smile spread across her face. Instead of tweeting back for all eyes to see, she decided to follow Dom so that they could Direct Message each other.

She sent Dom a DM that said *@DomtheKing I've been busy sorry I didn't hit you up. I'm back in Philly though.*

A few seconds later Dom replied, *@ModelLC Are you going to take me up on that dinner invite this time around?*

Lorraine thought about it and let the question marinate for a few minutes then sent a direct message back, *@DomtheKing I'm not really in the mood to eat and it's kinda late. How about we go somewhere for coffee or cappuccinos?*

As she was waiting on the message to come through Dom replied right back, *@ModelLC Ok that's fine with me. It sounds like you need more than coffee maybe a drink would be better.* She used all 140 characters and had to send another message, *@ModelLC let me know when you're ready...*

Lorraine quickly responded, *@DomtheKing You're right a drink is needed. Send me your address and I'll have my car service pick you up. I can't have you drinking and driving.*

Dom sent her address and Lorraine copy and pasted it into a text message to her car service and she also added, "Be at my hotel in 20 mins." then she sent the text.

Lorraine washed up and found something simple, but

fitting to put on. She wasn't really thinking about what she was doing, she was just doing it. She moved around as if she was floating. She was finally dressed in form fitting BCBG jeans, a tank top and some Prada sandals with a clean face and one layer of lip gloss on her lips. As she got in the car she asked her driver, "How far is the address from here?"

"It's estimated between twelve to fifteen minutes ma'am."

"Ok, thank you." Lorraine pulled her phone out of her clutch. She wanted to try to call Nasir for the third time.

"My pleasure ma'am," the driver said as he closed the door.

Nasir's phone rang a few times and then went to voicemail. *Fuck that! I'm not leaving his ass a voicemail; mutha fucka needs to learn how to answer my calls. Shit, what the hell would happen if I was dying and wanted to say I love you or tell him how I really felt one more time before I died. I wouldn't even be able to do that.* Lorraine thought shaking her head.

Thirteen minutes later they pulled up to a modern style house, it was a nice size in a quiet neighborhood. Dom walked outside when she saw the lights of the car pull up. "How are you doing sweetheart? It's good to see you again." Dom said giving Lorraine a hug and peck on the cheek. A weird feeling came over her and she shuddered from the touch of Dom's lips brushing against her cheek. "Um, I'm ok. I guess. I think I just need to get some drinks up in me and I'll feel much better."

"Ok. I'm going to get them for you as soon as we get to the lounge."

"The driver rolled down the divider and asked, "Where to next?"

Dom spoke up, "We're going to Industry XIX. Do you know where that is?"

"Yes, I believe I know exactly where that is; over on Chestnut Street, right?"

"Yep, that the one."

"Ok, it won't take long at all to get there." The driver said rolling the divider back up to give his customer and her guest some privacy.

Lorraine sat in place observing Dom. You could tell she was rough around the edges as far as her attitude. Not by the way she dressed, but more so by her facial expression that seemed to stay plastered on her face.

"Is that what it's going to be like—me doing all of the talking and you sitting back listening? You need the drink, so I want to hear what it is that's troubling you?"

"I'll loosen up when I learn a little more about you."

"Ok, well I was born in Philadelphia, but I have lived some of everywhere and I always seem to find my way back here. My mother was the type of woman to chase after a man. She needed a man to feel complete. If she met a man and he was here visiting, but she 'quote unquote' fell in love in however amount of time, she would pack up everything and move to his state and that's just how it was in my life as a child. When I was a teenager, I got tired of that shit and spoke up about it. Immediately, our mother and daughter relationship took a nose dive. It hasn't been the same since then."

"Wow, you've been through some things just like I have. Where was your father?"

Dom chuckled. "Where's my father, daddy, dead beat, sperm donor—I don't know, your guess is just as good as mine. When you find him, whoever he may be, let me know.

Shit, I probably done walked past my daddy a thousand times and I'd never know it."

The driver pressed the speaker button "We have arrived to your destination." He opened the door for them.

Dom was the first to exit the vehicle, she reached back inside and helped Lorraine out.

"Thank you, that's the type of thing my…well, never mind." she said looking away.

"Can you stay towards the front of the parking lot?" Lorraine asked.

"Yes I will ma'am."

"What drinks do you recommend?" Lorraine asked.

"Well, you look like more of a fruity drinker, but I think you need a strong, stiff drink at the moment, so not to take you too far out of your element, I'll order something in the middle of the two for you." Dom said taking the lead.

What the hell is going on here and why am I looking at her in this way? Lorraine wondered trying to check herself. *I love a man who can take charge and lead me in the direction I should go in without force, but she's a woman,* Lorraine thought, struggling to cope with her inner emotions. She was confused.

"Here you go. I got you a Dirty Martini and I got myself a Hole In One; no pun intended." Dom joked.

"Mmm hmm, I bet it's not." Lorraine said semi-flirting with her eyes.

"What else do you want to know about me? I want you to feel as comfortable as possible, so ask me anything and I'll tell you no lie."

"Ok, well I want to know when did you know you were a lesbian and why are you a lesbian?" Lorraine asked downing her drink.

"Damn, you took that like a G; let's move over by the bar so we can keep the drinks flowing and then I'll answer your questions."

Lorraine followed Dom over to the bar. She watched as every woman and some men, who were with a boyfriend, girlfriend, wife or husband, turn their attention to admire the women who, she figured they thought, were a beautiful lesbian couple.

"Yo' let me get two more Dirty Martinis and when you see an empty glass, just make another one. Keep 'em coming."

"I sure will sexy." The bartender, a short dark-skinned, petite chick responded.

Dom brushed it off like it was something she was used to. Lorraine was slightly offended. "Well damn, she's flirting with you all openly. What if I was your girlfriend? I would be in whoop a bitch's ass mode." She said feeling some type of way.

"Don't worry about that; I don't. I'm used to that type of forwardness from women." Dom said, immediately calming Lorraine's nerves and defusing the situation. "And plus, I'm with you right? So she can't compete even if she wanted to."

It was weird because had it been her and Nasir in the same situation, Lorraine would still be mad, fired up and ready to wreck some shit; but with Dom, it was the complete opposite. She didn't understand it. Maybe it was the drinks, but she was definitely feeling something for Dom.

"Now back to your questions. First I'm going to answer your question about why am I gay, which should answer your other question at the same time. I'm not gay because it's a trend or something I do for fun; this is me. I've never been with a dude before, but one of my mom's boyfriends touched me in the wrong way when I was twelve years old. He told me you're not gay, let me show you that you're not. He didn't get the chance to do anything to me because I kicked him right where his member hung. See at the time I had a girlfriend, he knew that because he had caught us kissing one day after school, but my mom didn't know at that time. I didn't understand the complete meaning of being a lesbian at that moment, but I knew that's what I liked. I stopped wearing girly clothes and started dressing in more baggier clothes so men wouldn't look at me in 'that way,' but it slowly became something that I liked to do. Men's clothes are way more comfortable."

"I'm sorry to hear that you had to go through that. It's interesting that you say you knew since you were younger that you wanted to be with females. I mean, I've never been with a female, but I've also never been completely pleased by a man. I'm starting to think something is wrong with me and not them." Lorraine was revealing more than she wanted to, but the drinks gave her loose lips and made her feel mellowed out.

"It's fine now. I used to have a girlfriend when all that was going on; she really helped me through everything. Now, about you never being completely pleased by a man… there is a problem there, but I don't think it's one that can't be fixed. So you think you're attracted physically to women?" Dom asked, pushing Lorraine further.

"What happened with you and this ex that you speak of? She seems like a good person to have stuck through that with you. And as far as my attraction…well, I think I'm attracted to females like you. Women that dress like men and have an aggressive, dominate persona. I've never acted on my curiosity because of my family and career. I mean what would people think?"

"I don't mean to interrupt, but here's another Dirty Martini. I see you're still on your first drink would you like another?" The bartender asked completely ignoring Lorraine's presence.

"I've been having an interesting conversation with my lady friend so I haven't had a chance to focus on my drink." Dom was cool until the bartender came over and made it known that she had barely touched her drink.

"That's fine." The bartender said sizing Lorraine up.

Who the fuck is this bitch looking at and why is she still standing here? Lorraine thought.

"Well, I have a question; are y'all here together and are you a man a woman?" She asked with no shame in her game.

Lorraine sucked her teeth. That was it, she had had enough. The liquor had her on a whole 'nother level. "Bitch, can't you see we're talking here. Back the fuck up, damn! You were going to get a nice ass tip, now you ain't getting shit! I know you gotta be friendly and flirt a little bit when you're a bartender, but you flirt with people who are by themselves, dumb ass." She said pointing her finger directly in the bartender's face.

"Oh, hell no! Security. Security!" The bartender walked off yelling.

"We gotta get up outta here." Dom said reaching in her pocket for money to pay the bill.

"We ain't gotta go nowhere. That bitch should've been more professional."

"It's not a good look to get kicked out of anywhere." Dom said as she held Lorraine up.

"Wait, let me at least finish the rest of my drink." she said gulping a full Dirty Martini.

They made it outside and to the car without incident. Lorraine was passed tipsy so Dom thought it was time to dig a little deeper. "What's going on with you and your husband?"

"Uh, I really don't know. He's not happy though he won't say it. I'm not happy, but neither one of us want to make the move toward a full out divorce talk. I'm not trying to have to split things fifty fifty. I earned all of my money; and I know he's not trying to split all of his with me."

"That's crazy because I'm a banker for a living, so I can make that problem go away. You will end up coming out on top with all of the money and happiness." Dom said trying to get Lorraine to take the bait that she was throwing out there.

"Really?" Lorraine asked excited. "I think I'm going to take you up on that because I deserve my happiness; and if that nigga is cheating, which I really think he is, he owes me for that and I want my pay in cash, not apologies."

"I'm going to make that happen for you, I promise." *For you and me.*

"I'm willing to make whatever you want or need happen; whether that's holding you, kissing you or both." Dom whispered, "I'll even kill your husband for you." Dom said staring deep into her almond shaped dark brown eyes. Lorraine looked away because her stare was too intense, too dark and too real. *Nasir dead...could we get away with it?* she wondered.

"If I find out he's cheating, then we will go to that extent; but if he's not, I'll just take the money. What I need from you tonight is just to hold me. Let me fall asleep in your embrace."

"Ok, I'm moving on your demand; so if that's how you

want to do it, that's how we're going to do it. Of course I will hold you all night for as long as you want me too." Dom replied laying her sweetness on thick.

"Ok, I like the sound of that."

Lorraine hit the speaker button to inform the driver that they were going back to her hotel.

Chapter Eighteen

I'm Free...Now Firsts Things First

Benzino was released from jail the day after Khia was shot and killed a couple blocks from the projects. He was at a loss for words when word got back to him that she had been murdered. He was listening to some young dudes, who weren't any older than nineteen, talk about the Shawty that got shot right on the street. He was used to people getting killed on the streets of Miami, but his attention was peaked when he heard the name, Khia, come out of one the youngin's mouths. They continued talking until they had flat out described Khia to a tea.

Benzino's main mission was to get some money quick, a whip and get to Atlanta as soon as possible. He didn't want to fly because what he planned on doing didn't need a plane ticket that could leave a paper trail right back to him. He knew Ty had something to do with Khia's murder; but he also knew she wasn't the one that did the killing—she didn't have it in her.

He had the information that Khia had given him while he was locked up. He knew he hadn't treated her like he should've the last time she visited him. His only option now was to make up for it by getting some answers and revenge;

both for her death and for his money that Ty had stolen—
over a million dollars. It never crossed his mind that Ty had
found or seen the DVDs of him with different drag queens.
His only thoughts were that she had crossed him. Because
Benzino didn't trust anyone, he never kept many people
around him; and the ones he did, did him dirty, took his cars
or ransacked his house, taking everything of value. Chris told
him that when he stopped by the house, no one was there; the
door was gapped open and the house was trashed. He was
hurting; and he only knew one person he could go to and ask
for the favor—an ol' head known as Pop in the hood, who
basically watched him grow up.

Pop gave him the money without questions, but he did
give him some key advice, *stay out of trouble youngin'. I
watched these streets raise you; I don't want to watch the
justice system kill you. Whatever it is you're about to do, get
in, handle your business and then get out; don't stick around
for too long.* Pop was a smart dude who once ran the same
Miami streets back in the day when the crime rate was way
higher than it is today. He had put in a lot of work cooked,
bagged and sold a lot of coke.

The ride to Atlanta didn't take nearly as long as Benzino
thought it would take. He stopped one time at a rest area to get
a few hours of sleep, a snack and then continued on with his
mission. When he arrived in Atlanta, he got a room, ordered
some Chinese takeout, relaxed, watched some TV and then
passed out; not realizing he had. When he woke up, it was
just after 11:00 p.m. Fuck man, I'm slippin'!" Benzino said
out loud. He splashed some water on his face and rubbed his
tired-looking red eyes. He knew he really should be getting
some rest, but he was too amped up on revenge to rest.

Benz didn't know Atlanta that well. He had made a couple trips there when he was first starting up his drug movement; he had wanted to tap into every part of the South that he could. A lot of people didn't know that he was the man behind the movement in previous deals, and as of lately, things had been slowing up. The stress had him reverting back to his old ways when he used to mess with transsexuals who look very close to a real woman. He used them to take his stress away; he'd been doing it ever since he was a teenager. When he first got locked up in an all-boys detention center, his first blow job was from a boy who was a couple years older than him.

During his entire ride over to what he thought was Ty's address, he thought about his younger years and how he'd gotten to this point in his life. There was no time to feel his heart beating now.

He drove the all-black sedan that he rented back in Miami to a couple houses down from the house he was looking for. *Look how good this bitch is out here living and I'm supposed to have some type of sympathy for her? She should've rode with me like she said she would.*

He got out of the car, checked his surroundings and then pulled the all-black mask and hoodie down over his head. He popped the trunk, pulled out a chrome and black .380 and connected a silencer. He didn't want anyone to get alarmed if they were to hear the gunshots, so he took extra precautions. He moved like a thief in the night, never in the same spot for more than a couple of seconds. He didn't notice any movement going on inside of the house that was the size of a mini mansion. By the time he reached the back of the house, he was covered in sweat. He readjusted his member in his pants because it was throbbing. It always got excited when he was about to kill. He would definitely have to find something to get into once he was done there.

Shit, I might get into this bitch before I sleep her ass for good. I bet she ain't even got an alarm since she's living in a nice neighborhood; dumb bitch.

He pulled the Dyno Kwick Lock Pick out of his pocket and used it as the sales person had told him to in the store. He was in the house within seconds. *I guess the shit is nicer on the inside. What the fuck did the bitch do, go and blow a half of mill on this house and it's décor?*

He made his way around the bottom half of the house, checking in every room, being as quite as possible. He cleared the bottom floor and then headed upstairs, only taking quick glances around the rooms with the doors open. The first closed door he got to he listened for a couple of minutes to see if there was any movement or noises coming from inside. *The Black Room? I wonder what goes on in the fuckin' black room.* He slowly opened the door and felt for a light switch at the same time; never taking his eyes off of the darkness. He hit the light and rushed in the room.

The room lit up red which he could see from the red light bulbs. It took a few seconds for his eyes to adjust to the lighting; once they did, he noticed a shape under the covers; he knew it was a body, but the body was way too big to be a woman's frame. His first thought was to shoot, but then he saw on the night stand a picture of a woman and a man on what he assumed was them on their wedding day.

Fuck, I done messed around and gone to the wrong house.

He felt his pocket where the paper was with the address and started to pull it out when the person in the bed started moving around as if they were waking up. He trained his gun on the individual, pulled the note out and repeated the address. He was definitely at the right house, but who were the people in the photo? He decided to find out.

"Alright mu' fucka, you done got enough sleep; wake yo' ass up." He said kicking the bed causing Nasir to jump.

"Aye man what the fuck is going on?" Nasir squinted. "What the fuck are you doing in my house?" Nasir's eyes got big at the sight of the gun pointed directly at his head. *Damn! The alarm. I forgot to set the fuckin' alarm!* "What do you want man? What can I do for you?"

A sinister smile appeared on Benzino's face. "Before I tell you what you can do for me I have some questions I need you to answer. Where the fuck is Tyquasia?"

Nasir's facial expression changed from blowed to confused by the mention of Ty's name. "Why are you checking for my shawty?"

"I figured you would ask that so I'm going to make this simple. I see your wife over there on that picture, it's nice to put a face with a name; Lorraine right? I would hate to have to hunt her down and dead her where she stands because her husband wants to play *super save a hoe* for his mistress. That's right; she's your mistress isn't she?"

Nasir ran his hands over his face. He was going to try the tough guy approach once again. "Look man, tell me what you want so that I can get it for you and no one gets hurt. Ty ain't got shit to do with the reason you're here. What? Did you follow me home after one of the parties I hosted and waited till the perfect time to make your come up? I'm telling you now bruh, I won't be your next come up."

"I knew you looked familiar and your name sounded too

familiar. You're that party promoter that comes to Miami all of the time. You host a lot of parties for celebs. I know who you are now. Ty is the main reason I'm here, and I'm not leaving until the bitch is dead. Now you can tell me what I want to know or I can go ahead and kill you now…no, as a matter of fact, I got some other plans for you. Get the fuck up!" Benzino ordered.

Nasir didn't move. He was calling Benzino's bluff. He didn't know who the dude was, but he wasn't about to let him come up in his shit and punk him. Benz noticed that Nasir wasn't moving or talking, so he decided to show him the shit was real. He moved the gun from pointing at Nasir's head and moved it to his left shoulder and pulled the trigger without warning. The bullet whistled through the air grazing Nasir's shoulder. He instinctively grabbed his shoulder to stop the blood from running. An inch to the right and Nasir probably wouldn't have a shoulder. Benz then repeated the same motion. He moved the gun to the right and fired it without warning, grazing Nasir's right arm. This time the shot knocked him back into a laying position. He had his arms across his chest, as if he was a mummy, as he tried to apply pressure to both of his wounds.

"Awh man, what the fuck did you do that for?"

Benz walked around the bed. "Now maybe you will take me a little more seriously. I'm going to ask you again, where is she?"

"I don't know where she is man; usually we meet up at the club and go to a hotel or some shit. She doesn't know where I live and I don't know where she lives. Ahh."

Benz chuckled. "It's funny that you say that, I wonder how someone who used to be close to her got this address. Ty took a lot of money from me while I was locked up. She left me and moved up here I guess to start a new life with you. She must've thought you were a good catch. Yeah, she loves a nigga with money. Since she cares so much about you, I'm about to make you hate your damn self. I wanna see what your head game is about."

Nasir looked like he'd seen a ghost. A tear finally rolled down his cheek. He knew that things wouldn't end well for him. What had he gotten himself caught up in by messing with Ty?

Benz pulled his sweat pants down to mid-thigh, exposing his already erect penis. "Looks like my man's here is excited. Bring your muthafuckin' head over here. You remember what happened the last time you didn't listen to what I said," he said gripping the gun tighter. Nasir moved his head closer, but left plenty of room between him and Benz. He was terrified. Benzino loved the look on his face, he grabbed his dick and proceeded to jack it and rub it across Nasir's lips. Some precum escaped the tip and landed on Nasir's top lip. Nasir couldn't take it anymore he threw up on the bed.

Benz had Nasir in a fucked up situation. "Awh nigga, quit being such a pussy; a little dick sucking never hurt anybody. Now open up. If you try some fly shit like biting my dick, I'm going to shoot your dick off and feed it to you." Nasir opened his mouth just a little. Benzino shoved his dick in causing Nasir to open his mouth wider and gag. "Now suck it! Remember…I can end your life at any time." Benzino said placing the barrel of the gun to Nasir's temple. The tears flowed freely as he was forced to do such a foul thing. He wouldn't wish this type of torture on any straight man. Once Benzino shot a load on to Nasir's face he was satisfied, but he decided to tea bag him for fun. He laughed the entire time while Nasir lay there stiff as a board as if death was knocking at his door.

He felt that he had demeaned him enough. He was through playing with Nasir and since he couldn't help him get to Ty, he had no real use for him. Benzino dragged Nasir down off of the bed by his foot. He struggled pulling him down the hall and when he got to the stairs, he didn't have the energy to pull him down the entire stair case so he gave him one hard kick which sent him tumbling down the stairs. When he got to the bottom of the stairs Benz pulled Nasir by his foot into the middle of the kitchen. He was breathing hard as he looked around the kitchen to find something that would cause Nasir excruciating pain. His eyes landed on the oven and that same sinister smile that appeared on his face before, appeared once again. He leaned over and punched Nasir repeatedly until he was almost unconscious. He then opened the oven and took the racks out.

Nasir's eyes were swollen closed, but he could hear the sounds of the racks in the oven being detached. He feared for the worst. Benzino folded Nasir's legs, breaking one of them so that the rest of his body would fit perfectly into the oven. Nasir moaned and blood seeped from his lips as Benzino took his time stuffing him, inch by inch, into the oven. He didn't know what he was going to do next, so he decided to play the waiting game.

Chapter Nineteen

Can't Nothing Stop My Happiness

Tyquasia was on an all-time high from the last two days that she'd spent with Nasir. He treated her like a queen. He cooked her breakfast, lunch and dinner; he ran her baths, made love to her, massaged her from head to toe and really made her feel like a woman is supposed to feel. She would've been with him tonight, but Paige had been blowing up her phone. She gave Ty a guilt trip about her not going to class or hanging out with her, so Ty had to make it up to Paige. They hung out the whole night, went to the movies to see the new Madea movie, bowling, and now they were having a sleep over at Ty's place.

"Ty, I never understood why you left Benzino when he got locked up? It had to be something big for you to just pack up and leave him without so much as a second thought." Paige said.

Ty took a long look at Paige because she knew she never wanted to discuss what made her leave Benz and move to Atlanta.

"I know you don't want to talk about it, but I really wanna know. We're besties and I wouldn't hide or keep anything from you."

Ty sighed. "Ok, I'll tell you, but after this I don't want to talk about him ever again. When he got locked up he told me that there was some emergency money in a safe in our master bedroom closet. From what we knew at that point, he was going to be behind bars for a very long time. He basically just wanted to make sure that I was straight during that time. He wanted to make sure that I had the money to hold everything down; bills, car and house maintenance, keep his canteen full and money on the phone while he was locked up. I was like, ok. Like any good girlfriend or wifey, I'm gonna hold my nigga down and be his ride or die. That was until I got to the muthafuckin' safe and found not just the money, but DVDs with different dates on them, some of the dates were within the last six months of that day. I bagged the money and took a couple of the DVDs to the home theater and popped one in. What came up on the screen will forever be etched in my mind." Ty said staring off into space, remembering that day as if it was happening all over again. "He was on the screen getting head and fucking a drag queen named Delicious."

Paige gasped. "Stop fuckin' lying. That nasty son of a bitch! I would've left his ass too, but not before burning down his house and telling his boys about their fudge-packing boss." she said just as mad as Ty.

"My point exactly; now you see why I don't want to just go around telling that shit to everybody with a damn ear. Just between me and you, I did put in a few calls to some close people of his, so I know they got the word out. That nigga is done for. He's washed up."

"You're not wrong at all girl, because like I said, I would've done that and some! What's going on with you and Nasir? What are y'all plans for the future?"

"Well, you know if it wasn't for you wanting to hang out

tonight, I would been with *my man*; but it's cool, I wanna make him miss me. He's home, knocked out in bed. I had to put it on him before I left because he did not want me to go. We're great though. He's happy, I'm happy and we're moving forward. We came to an understanding. He and his wife will be divorced very soon, so don't even form your lips to ask, 'Well, what about his wife' because we've got that covered."

"I was waiting on you to say something about a divorce. I can really and truly be happy for you guys now. If he's what makes you happy and he's going to do right by you I'm all for it; just remember that how you get the man is usually how you lose him. You got Nasir while he was married, so another woman may get him 'if and when' he marries you. I'm just saying; don't tear my head off for speaking the truth because I see how you're looking at me."

"I won't ever have to worry about that because unlike his current wife, I will be the one to keep him satisfied and happy. See that's where her problem came in—she didn't know how to be an all-around wife, but I do. Now, what I want to know is when is Ms. Paige going to settle down?"

"Honey, Paige is too young to be talking about settling down. I'm tryna have as much fun as I can now. I'll figure out the 'real relationship' thing at a later time. I'm in no rush, although there's a few prospects wanting and wishing to be the one to get me to settle down. It ain't happening until I'm ready; but it's fun to watch them try."

"I know that's right! Do it on your own time, that's when you'll know you're ready, because it's on your time and no one else's."

"Don't you think it's going to look suspect when you don't go to Khia's funeral? She was one of your best friends;

well' so you thought."

"I've already been through the fake reaction of hurt and sadness. My mother called me and broke the news to me while I was with Nasir, and boy did I put on. He held me as I sobbed. After a while, sobbing got tiring so I just sat quietly. I told my mother that I have finals and if I missed them I would fail the whole semester. Even though I'm failing already, she didn't need to know that. I couldn't go down there and pretend to be devastated for the whole time that I'm there."

"You know your ass is one of the best liars I know. I don't know how you do it with a straight face too." Paige yawned. "Oh shoot, I'm getting sleepy. This was fun."

"It's not hard. I've been lying for a long time and about a lot of things; but sometimes you gotta do what you gotta do. It's a dog-eat-dog world out there. My motto is, get them before they get you. Go ahead and go to sleep. We've been kicking it for a long time; it's about 5 A.M. right now. Shoot, I need to take my ass to sleep. I can't go without my beauty rest. I think I'll wake up later on in the morning, fix breakfast and call Nasir to come over."

"I feel you on that. It's definitely a 'get them before they get you' type of world; or at least that's how it seems. We *divaz* love our beauty rest and we must get plenty of it. See you in a few hours. I only eat turkey bacon and sausage— just a reminder. Night sweets." Paige said heading upstairs.

Chapter Twenty
Life Changing

After a drunken night including pillow talk, cuddling, and peaceful sleep, Lorraine didn't want to get out of bed because she knew that would mean that their time was coming to an end.

"What do you think about coming back to Atlanta with me for the weekend? I have an event today, but after that I'm free for the weekend. We can go to Vegas and just get away. I already know you don't work on the weekend, so that wouldn't stop you from coming." Lorraine said hoping that Dom would accept her invite.

Damn, I didn't see that coming; an invite back to the ATL with her. Hmm.

"If you don't want to come with me that's all you have to say instead of getting all quiet." Lorraine said, hurt by Dom's silence.

"Nawh, it's not that. I was just making sure there wasn't anything I needed to take care of this weekend, and since nothing comes to mind, I'm all yours." *Maybe I can make this bank transfer happen sooner than planned. Let me try my luck.*

"Yay, we're going to have an amazing time." Lorraine said kissing Dom quickly and then pulling away before she got too into it. She covered her face as if she was embarrassed.

Dom stood up in her sports bra and boxer briefs; showing off her face. "You don't ever have to be embarrassed when you kiss me. If you want to kiss me, kiss me."

Lorraine kissed her. At first she held back with the kiss, but as she got more into it she began to make love to Dom's mouth. It was the best kiss she'd ever had. It made her feel warm all over. "Ok, let's get ready to go because we still need to stop by your house. If I would've kept going with that kiss something was bound to get started up in here."

Dom chuckled. "The only reason I'm going to agree with you is that I know you have an event and I don't want you to be late. But rest assured if it wasn't for that—shit could've popped off all up and through here. It's been a minute for me; I don't just go around sleeping with different women. I like to keep it one at a time."

"Keep that thought, our time is coming."

* * * * *

Lorraine arrived back in Atlanta with minimum time to spare. She found her driver waiting for her with a sign that read, "Mrs. Cruz." *Not for long,* she thought

"Damn baby, slow down. The event ain't gonna be shit without you there." Dom said trying to keep up with Lorraine who was high stepping in her heels.

Lorraine had almost forgotten about Dom after they got off the plane because her mind shifted into business mode. She felt kind of awkward being with Dom out in Atlanta because everyone knew her and would surely be asking questions—speculating big time. Even though Atlanta is a city that is very open with their LGBT community, Lorraine didn't know how understanding her career would be of her future love life. It could either grow her career or damage it. A shell came over Lorraine and she was no longer the confident, sexy supermodel; she was now a nervous woman who feared what others would think of her. That is the same reason she didn't act on her curiosity in the past, because she worried what society thought about her.

"I'm going to take the car service over to the event. It's a good thing that you suggested I get dressed before we left. I still need to touch up my makeup in the car. It's not the point that the event won't be the same without me; it's the point that I hate being late to anything whether it's an event, photo shoot or hair appointment. I called my manager Nancy and had her send an extra car to meet me here. She asked a million questions and got no answers except that the driver was looking for a person named Dom. You can take the car over to a hotel of your choice and I will meet you there after the event. Go ahead and get your laptop setup so that we can start the transfers as soon as I get there." Lorraine rushed, talking at a mile a minute.

"Calm down. Everything is going to be fine. I'll see you after." Dom leaned in to give Lorraine a kiss, but she quickly turned her head leaving Dom with the option of kissing her cheek. Dom understood that public displays of affection for newly out-of-the-closet gay women was hard; so she kissed her cheek and headed over to the man holding up the sign with her name on it. Lorraine sighed a breath of relief and headed to her car. She touched up her make-up as best she could in the car and stepped out as if she'd just stepped onto the runway.

"I was getting worried. I didn't think you were going to

make it on time. You know this is an important event for the kids and you being the one announcing the auction items is really going to get a lot of these celebs to come out of their pockets. Look at you, you're glowing. Is it safe to say that you and Nasir are back on the right track? Never mind, we'll have plenty of time for girl talk later."

"I told you that I would make it on time, there was no need to worry. I wouldn't miss an event that benefits the kids. They fight a fight that I couldn't imagine fighting and they never show that they're letting the cancer get the best of them. Today we will get people to come out of their pockets; not only for the special edition LV bag and tie, but for the cause—the children. We don't need to discuss Nasir now or later." Lorraine stated, letting it be known that he wasn't the cause for her glow and current happiness.

Nancy looked at her shocked. "We don't have time for a cheating scandal. You're at the height of your career. You're married, so whoever this extra side person is, let it go." She growled through clenched teeth all the while keeping a smile on her face as the mayor approached. Mayor Ross was an older black man in his late fifties, but he didn't look a day over forty. He was tall and slim. He was a good looking black man who was maintaining his health well to still be looking that great at his age.

Lorraine brushed off what Nancy said. Not even acknowledging it. "Hello Mayor Ross, it's so nice to finally meet you. What a lovely event you and the city of Atlanta have put together for the Children's Cancer Research Center and charity. I love what it represents."

"Thank you Mrs. Cruz. What a pleasure it is to meet you as well. This is a great event that we do every year to raise money to keep the research center funded. Our hope is that one day they will announce that they have found a cure. We also give funds to charities that support the children with cancer who don't have insurance to cover their treatment and hospital bills. I just wanted to come to you myself and thank you for hosting the auction this year. It really means a lot when a celebrity of your stature takes time to do that. It shows that you're still humble." Mayor Ross said kissing Lorraine's hand.

If I'm not mistaken, I would say that Mayor Ross is flirting with me, Lorraine laughed to herself.

"Anytime. I am honored to be a part of such an event. I will do my best to raise the most money in the history of this auction. It's my hope that I will be invited back to do it all over again next year."

"We would love to have you back. I want you to go up there and do your thing. Make it original, own it."

"You bet Mayor," Lorraine said as she headed on stage. Nancy slipped her an opening speech that was prepared by her. Lorraine didn't have any time to write one, have it looked over and approved, so Nancy always made sure that she had one prepared for instances like this. The event was a success. Lorraine raised two hundred and fifty thousand dollars within the first hour. The highest amount of money raised in that amount of time by any auctioneer. She got to network and talk to a lot of people who she hadn't seen in years; some of them she went to school with and actually knew personally.

"Hey, do you want to go out for drinks later and have an old-fashion girl's night out like we used to do when I first became your publicist and before I was your manager?"

"Sounds like fun, but I won't be able to. I have some things I need to take care of and then later I'll be chilling with a friend who is in town."

"A friend, really? This friend must be Dom. How does he look?" Nancy asked being nosey.

"I really need you to go out tonight whether it's with some girlfriends or by yourself. Go out and find you somebody to get your freak on with. I need y'all to get it in all different type of ways. That way you'll be so stuck on him that you won't even think about my business." Lorraine laughed half way joking.

"Real funny. Go ahead and *chill* with your friend. I'll be alright and for your information...I get mine off whenever I feel like I want to."

"That's way too much information. Have fun with that toy that only goes buzzzzz at five different speeds, but can't ever hold a conversation with you." Lorraine laughed. "I'll catch you in a couple of days."

"Alright, don't be out there doing anything that I wouldn't; and if you do, please don't get caught. That'll equal more work for me and we both know I don't need that."

* * * * *

Lorraine called Dom to find out what hotel she was staying in. When she got to the hotel room Dom was sitting in front of the desk ready to work.

"It seems like it took you forever to get here. How did the event go?"

"The event was great. I hope they really find a cure for cancer because it's no joke. A lot of people that I talked to have had cancer affect them at some time in their life. It took so long for me to get here because I had to stop by the bank and get all of the information, the routing and account numbers. I don't just carry that type of information around with me."

"I feel you on that. It's good to hear that the event was a success like I said it would be. Now let's get to the business at hand. I need to set up the offshore Swiss bank account. Whose name will it be in? It can't be in yours because that can be traced. Whoever you choose, it has to be someone you trust." Dom said.

"Someone else? I would use my sister's information, but she tells her baby daddy everything and allows him to go through whatever he wants. If that nigga was to ever touch my money, I would have to kill his ass; so I can't use her. I love my manager to death, I trust her with my whole career, but that heffer would quit quickly if she had that type of money in her name. That's crazy I really don't have anyone that I can trust to have all of my money in an account with their name on it. Unless..." Lorraine started to say something, but stopped in her tracks to think it through.

"Unless what?"

"Unless the account is set up in your name. We will just stay around each other so that I know you're not trying to get missing with my money. If you do this I will hit you off with a lil' something on the back end after this is over."

"I would never runaway with your money without taking you with me."

"That's sweet and all, but I've seen money change people. They'll be talking one way one day and the next you won't even recognize the person in front of you."

"Although I don't put it out there and scream at the top of

mountains that I have a lot of money, I do. I'm well off. Like I was saying, some extra money isn't going to change that."

Lorraine smiled. "Ok, I can dig that. How long is all of this going to take? She asked taking a seat on the edge of the bed.

"It's going to take at least six to seven hours. First I have to set up a dummy account to route all of the money to, then I will set up the real account and route the money from the dummy account to the real account. Now I see how you're looking at me, but I'm making a dummy account so that if questions ever rise, which I'm sure they will, when the man finds out all of his money is gone he's going to blame his accountant for stealing it. That will cause an investigation which will lead to the dummy account. They won't be able to get any information from the accountant because none of the information is legit and they can't fuck with offshore accounts."

"Damn, yo' ass is packing some smartness, I gotta give it to you. You dot all your I's and cross all of your T's. Well, since it's going to take a while for all of this to go through, I'm going to head home and pack a light travel bag because I wanna shop in Vegas. I need to tell Nasir some BS like I have a gig that I'm flying out of town for. I had my driver swing me by a rental car place so here are the keys in case you need to go out and get something to eat or whatever. The car is in the garage. I'm going to take the car service to go home. I don't want you sitting up in this room the whole time I'm gone. We're in no rush to move the money so take your time; it's still going to be there."

Dom stood up and guided Lorraine over to her. "You know you're sexy when you give orders don't you? How sweet was that for you to think of me and rent me a car so I won't be stuck up in this room." She kissed Lorraine gently on the lips, then on the cheek and down to her neck, sucking lightly just to tease a little bit. "You better hurry back so that we can finish what I just started. I can bet you any amount of money that you're leaking right now as I speak."

"You knew exactly what you were doing sending me off all hot and bothered like this." Lorraine said smiling and blushing.

"Bring something sexy with you to wear when you get back. I want you to be my private model tonight."

"I sure will." Lorraine said as she left.

Dom grabbed all of the information that Lorraine had given her, her laptop, cellphone, keys to the rental and headed to the car. There was a lot that she already knew about Nasir. She had to send a warning to someone near and dear to her heart. She made the call, telling her there was an emergency and to meet her at Piedmont Park ASAP.

* * * * *

Dom sat at the park for a few minutes when a candy apple red 2012 Maserati Quattroporte pulled into the parking lot. She knew whatever nigga was riding behind the wheel had to have some cash. The car was sexy, she had to admit. Her eyes stayed glued to the car until the driver opened the door and out stepped a very gorgeous woman. She hadn't seen her in a while, but it was definitely her. Fly from head to toe.

She jumped up off of the park bench to meet her. "Damn beautiful, it's been a minute. I feel like you've been hiding from me. I've really missed you."

"Why would I hide from you D? Granted your ass is

crazy, you knew what the plan was…shit you came up with it. We're not supposed to see each other until everything has been handled so what are you doing here in Atlanta, you could jeopardize everything." Ty yelled.

Ty and Dom, aka D, have known each other since they were younger when Dom first moved to the Pork 'n' Bean Projects in Miami with her mother. She didn't talk to many girls or have many friends because none of them understood her tomboy way of dressing, but Ty liked it because she was different. She was attracted to her and Dom was in love with Ty at first sight, so in a short time they started dating. Spending time with Dom was easy when it came to Ty's mother; she saw the way Dom dressed, but she didn't care because in that day and age kids had their own styles.

Dom would go over Ty's house all of the time. She was the girlfriend who Dom had confided in when her mother's boyfriend fondled her. A year later, Dom's mother was moving on to another guy in another state and she had to move. Dom and Ty were hurt because they had been each other's first in everything and then they were forced to have a long distance relationship. They got to see each other about three times a year when Dom would come back to visit.

One year Dom came back to visit and Ty told her that she had an older boyfriend. When Dom found out who Ty's boyfriend was and what his status was in the hood she made a pact with Ty that she could continue dating him, but that they would drain his bank account while she was with him. They never took too much money out at one time, only a few thousand; nothing he would miss. Soon Dom became tired of sharing Ty with Benzino, so she set him up. While she was in Miami, she followed him around and watched his every move. When she thought it was the perfect time, she called the police and acted like an old woman telling the operator that there was a suspicious car riding around her neighborhood. She gave the license plates and description of the car to the operator and then acted like the phone disconnected. The narc that stopped him that day must've heard the call go out over the radio and was already in the area.

When Dom saw the cop put Benzino into the back of his car she knew that her job was done. She called Ty and told her that she saw Benz in the back of a police car. A couple days later Ty called Dom telling her about another dude that she'd met the night before. She told her who he was. Dom got on her investigative shit, finding out that he was big money and all of the money was legit. Dom devised a plan, leaving Ty to do the same thing she'd done with Benzino except this time it would be harder since he was married. Dom would have to play a role also; she knew just what role she would play when Ty told her that Nasir and Lorraine were having relationship problems.

"First of all, what did I tell you about always calling me D? I don't mind that shit sometimes, but lately that's all I've been hearing. You remember when I figured that shit out when we were younger that the only reason you gave me the nickname D was because you knew your friends would think D was a dude. You met me as Dom when we started dating at twelve. We don't have time to talk about that now though 'cause ya man Benzino is here and he's looking for you."

The look on Ty's face told it all, she was terrified. *Benzino's out of prison and in Atlanta looking for me? Oh shit!* "Tell me everything you know D."

"I know he ain't gonna fuck with you as long as I'm living and breathing. I got the word from that nigga Rex. Remember Rex? The one he beat up in front of the Bodega a couple of years ago? Well, that nigga been out for revenge ever since. This morning he called me and let me know that word on the block is Benzino got out yesterday and the first words that came out of his mouth were he needs to get to Atlanta to find you. The nigga went to Pop's shop and borrowed some money from him to rent a car so that he could get here. Now I've been in a lot of hoods and around a lot of bosses that have issued executions. Usually when you rent a car instead of flying somewhere you know that driving will take a long time to get where you are going; you drive so you won't leave a paper trail by buying a plane ticket. What that tells me is Benzino is here to kill you."

"Why is this shit happening to me? I told you D, once I took that money from the safe we should've got the fuck out of the country for a while. Now when I tell you about another nigga you wanna try to take him for all he got too. Now look at the fucked up position I'm in. I should've listened to my gut. By the way you're looking, I can almost tell that you're about to tell me some more bad news." Ty said, her confident swagga replaced by a defeated look.

"We can't talk about shoulda, coulda or woulda right now 'cause what's done is done. I am about to tell you some more bad news. When is the last time that you talked to Nasir?"

Ty just stared at Dom speechless. She wasn't worried when she hadn't heard from Nasir last night because she knew she had left him sleeping, but when she didn't hear from him anymore that day, she started to get worried and was on her way over to his house when she got the call to meet Dom at the park.

"You haven't spoken to him since yesterday, huh?"

Ty shook her head in agreement to what Dom was asking.

"Ok, well this morning after me and Lorraine landed, I had my driver take me by their house. Nothing looked suspicious until we drove pass their house. A couple of houses down, there was a black sedan parked with Florida license plates. I saved the license plate number in my phone and looked it up when I got to my room. The car comes back as being rented to Benzino which means he's there with Nasir, so Nasir is either dead or near death." Dom held Ty's hand. "Stay with me on this. I need you to drive over to a coffee shop close to their house that has Wi-Fi. I'm going to follow you there. It'll take me about ten minutes to put the information in for the wire transfer and get this money wire going. Once I'm done there, we will ride over to their house to watch the drama unfold from a distance. See, what Benzino thinks is that when you don't hear from Nasir you will go to his house looking for him, but what he doesn't know is that I have a plan for him. Let's go!"

Chapter Twenty-One

My World Is Crashing Down On Me

Nasir died during the night from his injuries, but that still didn't stop Benzino from doing what his sick twisted mind told him to do. He heard the car pull up, ran to the kitchen, turned the oven on to four hundred and fifty degrees and then slipped out the sliding glass door. He hurried to the front of the house just in time to see the woman from the picture in the bedroom hurry inside carrying luggage.

Damn it, I need to move a little faster. Slow ass driver, I didn't think I was ever going to make it home. I'm surprised Nasir's even here seeing how I just tried to call him and he didn't answer, Lorraine thought.

She kicked off her heels and picked them up to take them to her room with the rest of her luggage.

"Nasir where are you, you no good ass nigga? I've been calling your ass for three damn days and you didn't have the decency to answer the phone. The least you could do is help your wife with her luggage; don't you think?" She huffed, making it to the top of the stairs.

His ass must be out with that bitch he's been cheating on me with, but that's fine; I got something coming for his ass.

Lorraine went in to *The Black Room*. She took the big

luggage that carried most of her clothes and emptied it into the hamper. She went into her closet that she shared with Nasir. She picked out six basic things that every woman should take on a trip with them: a LBD—little black dress, a pair of nice fitting skinny jeans, a white tank top, a black and white Aztec print maxi dress, a blazer and a pencil skirt. She knew with those items, no matter where she went, she could be dressed up or dressed down for any occasion. Next she moved over to the shoes. She had so many choices it would take forever to decide which to take, so she went with basic colors. She got a pair of nude pointy heeled pumps, a black pair of stilettos, and some sandals for when she wanted to dress casual. She chose a sexy lingerie set that she knew Dom would love. It was completely sheer, leaving nothing to the imagination. She also grabbed a few extra pairs of thongs because she knew messing with Dom she would need them. She was ready for whatever was to come, she was excited. Just as she was zipping up her luggage she got a whiff of what smelled like death mixed with burning wood. Before she knew what was going on, the fire alarm started blaring throughout the house.

That bitch got his head so fucked up he done left some fuckin' food in the oven cooking. Now what would've happened if I wasn't home, our whole house would've gone up in flames behind this wet dick ass nigga chasing after a big booty, no name, ratchet mistress, Lorraine thought as she made her way downstairs.

The living room was filling up with smoke. She ran through the living room and into the kitchen. Something was wrong. The house just didn't feel right. *Maybe I didn't notice it when I first got here because my mind was so focused on getting back to Dom, but I feel it now, something is wrong here.*

When she got to the kitchen she was apprehensive about going all of the way in. She stepped in and saw that sparks were coming from the top of the stove. She wanted to try to turn it off. *Fuck this shit, I'm calling 911 and letting the professionals deal with this shit.*

Lorraine tried to run out of the kitchen and ended up slipping and falling into some hot reddish brown liquid that was running from the oven. She reached up and grabbed the oven's door handle to pull herself up, but slipped back down; pulling the door open and revealing its contents as she slipped. She covered her mouth as the tears streamed down her face.

"Nasir!" She said in almost a whisper.

She got up slipping and sliding in a panic. "Oh my God! Who did this to you? Ahh!" she screamed. She ran to the living room visibly shaken. She grabbed the house phone trying to steady it in her hands as she dialed 911.

"911, what's your emergency?" The operator came on after the first ring.

"My...my...husband is...dead!" she said nearly inaudible.

The kitchen engulfed in flames.

"What is your address ma'am and I need you to speak up, I can barely hear you."

Lorraine gave the operator her address as best she could while grabbing her purse to run outside.

"Help is on the way. Can you tell me how do you know your husband is dead?" The operator asked.

"Because I just came home and found him in the fuckin' oven cooking. Ok. My damn house is on fire can you tell them to hurry up." Lorraine snapped, feeling as though she was losing her mind and that the world was crashing down on her.

"Ma'am, I need you to remain calm. You should hear the sirens from the emergency vehicles coming down your street. They will be to you any second."

That's all Lorraine needed to hear before she hung up in the operator's face.

* * * * *

Ty pulled over as the ambulance and fire truck went blaring down the street whizzing passed her towards Nasir's house. *Damn, he really got to him. This is all my fault. Now D's crazy ass has another plan.*

"She must've found him. Alright time to spring into action. Pull up a couple houses down from theirs, in ten minutes you're going to call 911 from this disposable phone. Tell the operator that Lorraine Cruz killed her husband. When the operator asks you how do you know that act like the line is breaking up. Once you do that, I'm going to get rid of that phone. Now I know Benzino is around here somewhere watching to see how things play out. I want you to get out of the car in plain view and act as a spectator watching from a distance. Don't worry, I don't think he's that damn crazy to try and kill you in front of all those witnesses and the police."

Ty listened to Dom and wondered how she'd let herself get into this situation. She really loved Dom deeply, but her way of thinking was really fucked up.

"Once this is all over promise me that we'll leave the states for a while and take an extended vacation."

"If everything goes the right way, I promise we'll get out of here." Dom said giving Ty a little bit of security.

Ty drove a couple houses down from Nasir's house where she could see the smoke coming out the top of it. She got out of the car with the disposable phone and she dialed 911. When the operator picked up, she told her that the woman who'd just called in had murdered her husband. She gave the operator Lorraine's full name and address. Ty let her know that the fire and rescue squad was at the house. She told her that they better arrest her now because she was planning on running. The operator started asking her questions about who she was and how she knew all of the information that she was giving.

Ty said, "Ma'am, I have to go because if y'all don't arrest her she's going to come after me because she knows that I know what she did. I know what I know because she told me so. I'm scared for my life, I shouldn't even be talking to you." Ty hung up the phone. She looked at the neighbors starting to gather around at the end of the driveway; she saw one person who looked really familiar. *Benzino.* Their eyes met at that very moment. Ty's heartbeat sped up and her stomach felt as though it had formed into a knot. A cold sweat came over her as she stared into his dark eyes. He looked at her with a crooked smile, winked and then held up his index and middle finger together, pointed them at her making a shooting gesture. She watched his lips moving, he was saying, "Pow! Pow!" Repeatedly.

Awh shit, this crazy mutha fucka really stuck around like D said he would. I wonder what he has planned for me.

She tried to show no fear. She poked her chest out straightened up her posture and got back inside the car. When she looked back in that direction Benzino was gone.

"He saw me and I saw him. He's still here." Ty said.

"I figured that. I want you to drive slowly by the crime scene. When he sees your car he's going to follow us, except he won't know I'm in here. Your tank is full so we can take that bitch nigga for a ride." Dom said adjusting the passenger seat so that it would lay all the way back.

Ty started the car and drove toward the crowd. As she eased by, she looked up the driveway to see Lorraine handcuffed and being escorted to an awaiting Crown Vic. The detective placed her in the back of the car and then got in the driver's seat.

"He's probably taking her in for questioning. Hopefully, we'll have one situation handled for us, or they may let her go 'cause she's the loose end."

Ty continued driving. "Where am I going?" She asked thinking about how every time she was around D she brought out a submissive side in her that never seemed to be there when they weren't around each other.

"Just keep driving, I'm looking up a location now. Bingo! We're going over on Tulane Drive, South West Atlanta."

Driving over to Tulane Drive, Ty's mind was going a mile a minute. She wanted to know how it would all end. Every couple of minutes she looked around, checking the rearview mirrors—paranoid. There he was, a ways back, probably so he wouldn't spook her, but she was already on to him.

"He's following us now. A couple cars back is that black sedan you told me he was driving."

"Yeah, I peeped that a few lights back. Turn left right here. Keep a steady speed, I don't want him to know that you're on to him."

Ty made the left. The sun was going down and the road they were driving down didn't have any lighting. Dom sat up just enough to see out of the rearview mirror, but not so much that you could see her head visibly in the car.

"Make a right up in that parking lot, drive around back and kill the lights."

"What is this an abandoned warehouse?"

"Yeah, it's a warehouse I found it on Google. It's been abandoned for a few years. He just pulled in, I saw his lights. Be very quiet, I need to hear if he gets out of the car. Keep your foot on the gas and be ready to go when I say go."

The minutes that passed by felt like time stood still because nothing was happening not a sound was made.

* * * * *

Benzino got out of the car leaving the engine running. He knew he'd seen Ty pull into the parking lot. *Now the little bitch wants to play games,* he thought. That only further fueled his anger. He walked to the back of the parking lot and was rounding the corner of the warehouse where he came face to face with a car coming at him full speed; he didn't have time to react. He couldn't see the driver because the lights were turned off on the vehicle, but he knew Tyquasia was behind the wheel. He stood there showing no fear. He wasn't about to let a bitch pump fear into his heart and he knew Ty didn't have it in her to hit him. At the last minute the lights came on and he saw a passenger smiling at him. Her face forever etched in his mind. He tried to pull his gun right as the car hit him sending him air bound. He hit the ground with a loud thud sound. Dom got out of the car and stood over Benzino. She wanted to see the pain on his face up close.

"Fuckin' dyke bitch! I knew y'all were fuckin' the whole

time, I just couldn't prove it. I kept asking that triflin' bitch."
He coughed up blood. He touched his legs. "I can't feel my
legs; you bitches done paralyzed me. Tell her to come and
see what she did to me."

As he spoke the words, Ty walked up to him.

"Oh, so I'm a triflin' bitch, but you were the mutha fucka
fudge dippin' with men dressed like women all up and through
Miami; you nasty, pine dick dog, water cum-shooting piece
of shit." She screamed and spit on him. "You thought you
had something for me huh? Well check this out." She raised
her six-inch stiletto about to smash it into his face, but Dom
stopped her.

"You never kick the enemy while they're down. I know
you can think of something better, can't you?"

A slick smile appeared on Ty's face as she walked back to
the car. "Back up baby. I got something for his shitty dick ass."

Dom took the disposable cell phone out of her pocket,
wiped it off and stuck it in Benzino's pocket. She stepped
back.

Ty got in the car, put it in drive and proceeded to drive
directly over him. The left front and rear tires crushed his skull
instantly, and the right wheels broke his legs and smashed his
knee caps to fragments. She didn't stop there, after she rode
over him the first time she drove up some stopped, put the
car in reverse, accelerated on the gas and rode over him again
like he was a speed bump in the middle of the road. If she
could, she would've rode back and forth over him until he
was smeared into the concrete and gravel.

"That's the type of shit I like baby. You know when you
let that inner lioness out I get turned on. Damn, you're sexy
when you're mad. I'm about to take his car and let it roll right

down that embankment."

"I hate to go there, but he took me there. Trying to come for me, mutha fucka can't come for me!" Ty had some renewed confidence now that Benzino was taken care of. "Hurry up and do what you gotta do so we can get out of here."

Ty watched as Dom drove the black sedan rental to the edge of the embankment. She got out wiped it clean, picked up a two by four and wedged it between the back of the seat and the gas petal. The car sped up and crashed down at the bottom of the embankment.

"What's next genius? We have one problem solved now what are we going to do about the other one?"

"I'm hoping that, that problem will solve itself. Let's head back to your place, I need to see what the news is reporting."

Chapter Twenty-Two
I Can't Tell You What I Don't Know

Lorraine sat in an interrogation room being asked the same questions for the last two hours. There was one older Latino detective who went by his last name Vargas. He kept a smug look plastered on his face. He wasn't buying shit that Lorraine was saying and he was watching her closely on how she reacted to every question. His partner, detective Hamilton, was more of the quiet type, only speaking up when she felt that Vargas was being a little too hard on Mrs. Cruz.

"When I sit here and look at you Mrs. Cruz, I don't see some weak woman. You're tall and petite, so I think to myself how could this petite woman get her husband into an oven?" He paused to let that marinate. He then yelled, "I'll tell you how...the only answer that comes to mind is you didn't do this alone. Hell, I'm even willing to give you the benefit of the doubt and say you were forced to do it. However it happened, I know you had a part in the gruesome killing of Nasir Cruz." He pointed his finger in Lorraine's face; she was distraught, confused and broken.

"Alright Vargas calm down, that's enough now. Let's give her a break and then come back and talk to her after we've all had a chance to take a breath and clear our minds." Hamilton said patting her partner on the back.

"Yeah, I'll give you a few minutes to get your thoughts together and come up with another lie. The one you are telling about being at an event and then after leaving that event you were with a mystery woman who you only seem to know by the first name of Dom, makes no sense to me." Vargas said storming out of the interrogation room.

"I didn't kill him, he was my husband. I didn't have a reason to hurt him." Lorraine cried out. She was shaking un-controllably.

"Yo' man, you got to calm down in there. How do you expect to get a confession out of her with you all down her throat? Honestly, I don't think she did it. You saw the size of that man; even halfway burned up you can tell he was a well-built man. She couldn't have put him in there by herself. She would've needed help." Hamilton said.

"I don't care what you say. You're only siding with her because it's the soft side in you. You're a woman, you don't see what I see."

Hamilton cringed when Vargas said that. She hated when her sex was thrown up as an excuse of right from wrong.

"You saw the bags packed in their bedroom. Maybe she didn't think he would catch on fire so fast. I'm going back in there and this time I'm not coming back out without a confession or a name of her accomplice."

Hamilton shook her head. Something wasn't sitting right with her, but she knew once her partner's mind was made up there was no changing it.

* * * * *

Dom grabbed the remote control as soon as she got in

Ty's apartment and then plopped down on the couch. She cut on the TV and started flippin' through the channels.

"Ty what are the news channels here? I can't find not even one news station."

"There's a lot of them: Fox5, WSB-TV2, and 11Alive are the ones that come to my mind right off the bat."

Dom changed it to each channel until she found the one that was on the story she wanted to hear about.

"Hello, this is Steve Anderson reporting live with Fox5 in front of the Cruz's residence. Where just three hours ago, Lorraine Cruz, a high-fashion model know throughout Atlanta, was taken down to homicide. The police are not releasing a lot of information at this time, but it is confirmed that the very popular promoter and host, Nasir Cruz, is indeed dead. Hold on, I have reports coming in at this very moment." The newscaster said listening to every detail coming through his ear piece.

Dom and Tyquasia looked on watching intensely.

He screwed up his face. "Hold on, let me make sure I'm hearing this right. Mrs. Cruz just admitted to killing her husband and is willing to write a sworn statement saying so?" He said more as a question than a statement. "I was just interviewing her at the cancer fundraiser a few hours ago, now this."

The cameraman cleared his throat. "We're still live on air, the camera is recording."

"Oh shoot. Umm…we will be right back with further updates."

Ty sat there with a confused look on her face, while Dom had a big goofy smile on her face.

"Why would Lorraine admit to killing Nasir when she

really didn't do it."

"If what that reporter just reported is true, they must really be giving it to her in that interrogation room. See baby, let me explain something to you. I've been in one before with two of the nastiest detectives in Philly. The way that they play good cop, bad cop is crazy because you think one cop is on your side and understands what you're saying and that the other cop is just mean and not trying to hear what you have to say. Shit, reality is that the one playing good cop could care less what you have to say, just as long as you admit that you did it regardless if you did or didn't."

"Damn, that's crazy! I guess that means we can wrap up here. I'll put my furniture in storage, pack my things so that I have things to take with me to a beautiful island somewhere far away."

"Not so fast baby."

Ty looked at Dom like she had three heads or something.

"I know you want to go and relax, trust me I do too. We deserve some quality time spent together enjoying each other; but we can't just pack up and leave. We have to see this through because if that report is false, but they see her as their main or only suspect, then there will be a trial and we need to be here for it to make sure that she gets one verdict and one verdict only—Guilty."

Ty looked disappointed, but she knew what Dom was saying was the right thing to do.

"Bring your sexy ass over here."

Ty sashayed over to where Dom was sitting on the couch. She straddled Dom.

"I don't ever like to see my lady looking sad or disappointed, so tell me what I can do to make it better for now."

"Hmm, for starters you can come take a hot steamy candlelit bath with me. Let's talk money and numbers. You know that always gets my juices flowing and then you can top it off by giving me some monster head with a side of bang my back out."

"I got you covered in all areas." Dom replied kissing Ty's perfectly shaped lips.

"You always know the right thing to say. Let's head on upstairs and get started right now."

"I'm right behind you."

* * * * *

Lorraine was over the interrogation. She'd lost her mind and was no longer thinking logically. The constant back and forth bickering between the two detectives and the images that kept flashing in her head of Nasir folded up in the oven burning every time she would blink her eyes were horrible and taking a toll on her. What had she done to deserve this type of treatment? She couldn't take the questioning about problems in their marriage; was he cheating or was she cheating? She was sick and tired of being sick and tired; she did the only thing she knew would make it all go away at least for the moment. "I did it, ok, I did it. Is that what you muthafuckas want to hear?" She spat with rage in her tone and showing it in her eyes.

Vargas looked at his partner to make sure he'd heard right. With a smile slowly creeping across his face he asked, "Can we get a written confession with full details?"

"Yes." Lorraine whispered.

Hamilton shook her head in disbelief.

Vargas wasted no time pulling out a legal pad and pen,

placing them in front of her. Lorraine stared at the pen and legal pad not knowing what she was going to write.

"I need some time to myself." Lorraine whispered.

Vargas nodded his head at Hamilton and they left the room.

"Great work on getting the wife to confess, I knew something wasn't right about her story at the scene." Parker said.

Vargas slapped hands with Parker. "I know, right man! I was reading through that fake sobbing and story from the moment I saw her. Hamilton is the only one that believes her. It's a woman thing though; you know how that goes." Vargas said sharing an inside department joke with Parker.

"Whatever, you two fools!" Hamilton said.

They went to another room a few doors down that looked like a conference room with a small television on the desk. Vargas cut on the monitor and sat back to watch Lorraine. Hamilton stood there shaking her head.

"She's a beautiful woman right?" Hamilton asked.

"Yes, I must admit she is really a nice looking woman."

"What nice looking woman do you know that will fold their fine, successful husband up, breaking his bones and all, and put him in an oven, turn it on and cook him like he's the main dish at Thanksgiving dinner?" Hamilton asked.

"A woman scorned will do anything. I'm willing to bet that Mr. Cruz was cheating on her and she found out. I think that's what she is—a woman scorned. She got caught up in her emotions and didn't think before she acted."

"Ok, even if I agree with you on that, how did she knock him unconscious to be able to put him in the oven; surely if he was conscious he would've put up some type of fight."

"I don't know. I can't answer that for you, only she can."

Vargas replied, tapping on the screen. "She's starting to write; see…I told you she's confessing."

They looked on as Lorraine wrote on the legal pad. They couldn't see exactly what she was writing, but they still looked on. After a few minutes, she put the pen down and turned the pad over.

Vargas scrunched up his brows. "She's done already? What type of detailed confession is that? I did it, the end?" He wasn't happy, so he got up to head back into the interrogation room.

"Done already are we?" Vargas asked upon entering the room.

Lorraine simply turned her head away and wiped away the tears that flowed down her face.

Vargas picked up the notepad and turned it over. In big letters were the words:

FUCK YOU! I WANT MY LAWYER…
Signed,
The Innocent Bitch

"I see we have a smart ass here aye? Ok, we can play that game."

"Detective Hamilton, can you get forensics down here to collect Mrs. Cruz's clothes since they're covered in blood? Also make sure she gets one phone call to her lawyer." He said before staring her straight in the eyes. "You're going to need your lawyer because you're being placed under arrest for second degree murder." Vargas left out of the room leaving Hamilton to deal with Lorraine.

V. Brown

*****

The next day Lorraine had a bond hearing to see if she could get out on bond. Her lawyer, Chanda Freeman, informed her that most of the evidence they had was circumstantial and could go either way in the courtroom if the case was to go to trial. The judge set Lorraine's bond at one million dollars. She was relieved that she was finally able to get out of that hell hole; or so she thought.

"I will be there to pick you up as soon as I go to the bank and pick up the money for the bondsman. Once the bond has been paid, it's just a waiting process of all the paperwork between the courthouse and jail being filled out and processed; and once that's done, you will be out." Chanda said.

"Thank you so much for everything Chanda. I didn't know who else to call. I know you're busy with other cases, but I was going crazy. I can't wait to get out of here and take a hot steaming shower and scrub all of this jail house smell off of me." Lorraine quivered.

"Speaking of my other cases that I'm working on, all of those clients are paying so I'm sure I will be able to pick up my retainer fee with your bond money at the bank right?" Chanda asked.

"Yes, you will be able to pick it up. I signed the authorized document that you gave me for you to have access to my private bank account, so do what you have to do to get me out of here ASAP!" Lorraine replied zoning in and out.

"That's all I needed to hear; I'm going to take care of that part right now. I will see you soon. Keep your head up for only a few more hours."

The next day.

When the guard came to Lorraine's cell she thought it was time for her to leave the jail; instead the guard told her she had a visitor. She was confused, but followed him to the visitation room. It was Chanda and she was sitting in her seat with her arms folded across her chest. She didn't look like she was in a good mood which further fucked up Lorraine's thought process.

"How are you doing today Lorraine?"

"I'm not too good. I thought I would've been getting out yesterday, at the latest this morning, but I'm still here in this washed-out jump suit."

"You've known me for some time now, so I'm sure you know that my time is valuable and I hate for it to be wasted. I stopped working on other cases to do this for you. Tell me why when I went down to your bank yesterday after leaving the courthouse with a smile and signed authorized papers to withdraw the money, the bank teller looked at me funny when she went into your account. I asked her was there something wrong and she said that she wouldn't be able to withdraw any money. You know me, I put on my *and why is that* face. She broke it down to me as simple as it gets. There wasn't any money to withdraw. The bank account was on E. I told her there must be some mistake because my client is a high-paid fashion model who makes plenty of money and there is no way that her account should be empty. She called her manager over who went into the account to check the history, and low and be hold all of the money was transferred out the account the same day that your husband was murdered. I don't know what kind of game you're trying to play, but I don't want any part of it. Since I was never actually appointed as your attorney, I will discontinue my services in this case

as of five minutes ago. You try to enjoy the rest of your day."
Chanda pushed her chair back and stood up straightening out
her Prada pant suit. She turned on her five-inch heels and
walked off.

Lorraine was left speechless. All of her money was gone
from the private account that she started when she first got
her big modeling deal.

Dom, she thought. *How could I forget what we were
supposed to be doing? Oh my God, she must've went through
with it even after she didn't hear from me. She's probably
somewhere enjoying all of my fuckin' money.*

That may have been the straw that broke the camel's back
because the room started to spin and Lorraine had a shortness
of breath like someone had some powerful hands around her
neck squeezing it. She passed out, bumping her head on the
table.

Lorraine learned that she had, had an anxiety attack. She
had held her breath without knowing it and the lack of oxygen
caused her to pass out. The doctor explained that to her in the
infirmary when she woke up.

Chapter Twenty-Three

Is This The End?

Ty was aggravated because the last couple of days all she and Dom seemed to do was sit in the house with the TV on whatever channel was talking about the Cruz murder. It's like Dom had become obsessed with the murder. She wanted to know every detail.

"Baby, don't you wanna get out of the house for some fresh air, maybe go somewhere to get a bite to eat?" Ty asked rubbing Dom's curly mini fro that had begun to grow since she hadn't gotten a hair cut in a while.

"Not right now bae. We can go out as much as you want…"

"When this is all over." They said at the same time.

"Don't be like that, I mean it. How many days ago was it that the judge awarded her a bond? She still isn't out yet, so I guess that means she didn't find anyone to get the money from."

Ty sucked her teeth and walked off, she didn't want to talk about the case anymore. She did the only other entertaining thing she could think of, read a book on her Kindle. She'd become used to using her Kindle for the last week. All she did was read. There was a new author out that was bringing that heat. Her name was Blaque. Ty went to Amazon and 1-clicked all of her titles after she read her first book *Exhale*.

Three weeks later there was still plenty of talk about the *Cruz Roasting Murder* as the news named it. Lorraine was physically and emotionally drained, within the two weeks she'd met her new court-appointed public defender, she had been to court twice to get a trial date for the second degree murder charge she faced; but both times her court date was pushed back. She was out of her mind; barely eating the slop that they served at breakfast and dinner. She was losing weight slowly, but surely. She was really ready for the whole nightmare to be over.

One particular day Lorraine was sent to solitary confinement for trying to choke another inmate. The woman had been taunting her about Nasir's death for several weeks. Every day, the woman would sit around with her friends and talk about Lorraine out loud so that she could hear them. They laughed at how they felt she was stupid for killing a man as fine as Nasir. When Lorraine finally said something back to the jailhouse bully, letting her know she didn't do it, the woman joked, "First you say you didn't do it, then you did, now you didn't again. I told y'all this bitch was crazy. A fuckin' looney bin. I don't know what he saw in your ass anyway. You're just as tall as a bean stock and you barely got meat on your bones, a little ass, small tits; he must've been cheating on you with a bad ass thick chick that's why you killed him. She was prettier than you. Yeah, that's what it was." She laughed high fiving her home girls.

The other inmates gathered around. One spoke up. "Yo' don't let her talk to you like that." But she was quickly quieted when their eyes switched to her and she was now the target.

"Let that go honey. Them young girls don't know any better." An older woman with cornrows said to Lorraine.

Lorraine's head started spinning and she couldn't control it, her vision went red and she snapped. She stood up, jumped across the table where they were eating, picked up her tray and smashed the loud mouth bully right in the face. She dropped the tray and started punching her; every punch was heard loud and clear. Lorraine was breathing like a beast. The woman tried to fight back, but she was no match for Lorraine. Her friends, who were with her, stood back and watched; not wanting to get involved in the one-sided fight. "You done fucked up now you prissy bitch, you won't be able to walk around here much longer." One of the inmate's friends yelled out.

"Not alive anyway." Another one added.

"Man Shalonda, you were supposed to beat the breaks off that bitch coming at you like that. You know you are top dog around here…well, at least you were. This jail shit is just a pit stop for you, you better get her back before you head back to prison 'cause if them girls up the road find out about this, all of your credibility is going to be questioned for letting this husband-killing model bitch beat your ass!" A chubby, manly-looking inmate yelled.

Lorraine slammed Shalonda's head on the floor when the first set of guards bum-rushed her. Blood was leaking everywhere from Shalonda's mouth, nose, and from a cut above her eye. The guards tackled Lorraine to the floor.

"It wasn't me, it was her. The bitch kept fucking with me and pushing me. Enough was enough."

The manly-looking chick mouthed the words, *you're dead* and swiped her hand across her neck like she was dragging a knife. Lorraine put her head down because she had nothing left. The woman was right, she was dead.

Shalonda spit out blood while she was being cuffed. "Your days are numbered. You better hope one of us leaves here soon. Whether it be me going back to prison, or you going to trial and being found 'not guilty'; whatever the case is, your ass is mine up in here. Believe that!" Shalonda said through clenched teeth.

"Alright Peterson, enough with the threats," a CO that Lorraine had seen previously joking with Shalonda on numerous occasions said. Two guards drug Lorraine off to solitary confinement.

* * * * *

Try being locked away in solitary confinement for a week staring at four bare walls; not being able to see or feel the sun on your skin, peeing and shitting in a drain in the corner or the room, being fed what looked like dog food, but smelled like horse shit—that's what Lorraine endured. She was willing to do whatever she could to be taken out of her misery. She went to sleep and woke up wishing that she didn't wake up.

The slot on the door slid open and something was pushed in and then the slot was slid closed again. Lorraine sat there just staring into space. She was out of touch with reality. She didn't know what day it was or what time it was. She began to feel around for whatever had been pushed in. Her finger came across something small. She felt around on it. "Ouch." She said when she pricked her finger on the razor. She stuck her finger in her mouth to suck up the blood.

The thought entered her mind and she tried to push it out, but it was too late. She was convinced that, that was the only way out of her current situation. She put the razor to her thin wrist and guided it across—lightly opening her skin, but not causing much pain. She said a prayer as she did it again because she liked the electric feeling she felt shoot through her body when the razor cut through her skin. *Lord forgive me. I have sinned. I wasn't always perfect, but I tried my best to be as close to perfect as perfect gets. I know I didn't succeed, but I hope you welcome me home with open arms and know that I was just a broken soul. Nasir, I'm coming to you. I hope you forgive me for whatever part I may have played in messing up our lives. I didn't have the chance to be the woman you needed me to be, but I will be in heaven. Meet me at the gates.* She used the razor again and again; each time cutting deeper and deeper until she'd cut straight through her veins—killing herself instantly.

Chapter Twenty-Four

The End All That Be All

Ty had been packing and getting everything in order for when it was time for
them to leave and take their extended vacation. She'd already
hired a company to move her furniture into storage and all of
her clothes were packed and ready to be shipped to the first
location that they would be heading to.

"That's it, it's a wrap baby. It's all over. She just killed herself in solitary confinement the news reporter just said it." Dom
ran in the room yelling.

Ty was less enthusiastic. "Babe, don't play like that, you
know how ready I am to go. Don't come in here joking around."

Dom walked over to Ty's plasma TV and cut it on. "Listen
to this. He's talking about it right now. He's saying how it's
such a crazy ending to a weird turn of events. He said that
Lorraine had lost her mind in jail after she found out she was
broke and that her case would be going to trial. The judge kept
pushing the court date back which probably sent her over the
edge."

"Oh my goodness! How did she kill herself?" Ty asked
with her hand over her mouth.

"The report says that she sliced her wrist open killing
herself instantly when she cut through her vein. They don't

know how or where she got the razor from, that's still being investigated, but now the murder case is closed. She was the only suspect."

"It's over, it's really freaking over." Ty said smiling. She hadn't been this happy in a while. "So when are we leaving?"

"As soon as I get packed up we can go. I've already made plans for my best friend to live in my house in Philly, so she's going to be holding it down while we're gone."

"Well, I guess we're getting on the next thing flying out 'cause the clothes you brought from Philly I washed and folded them. They are packed and ready to be shipped with my clothes. It's not like you're going to need them 'cause there will be a lot of shopping going on during this trip."

"I'm also going to find some stocks and stuff that I can invest our money in so that we can start making more money." Dom added with a smile.

"You can take care of the investing and I will take care of the spending." Ty smiled back, kissing Dom on her lips. "You're going to get it you know that right? I'm gonna have ya world fucked up. You won't know if you're coming or going."

"Mmm hmm, not if I fuck your world up first. We won't make it to the airport if you keep on."

That calmed Ty down quickly, nothing was stopping her from going on her extended vacation starting in Saint Tropez. They took a cab to the airport. Ty decided to rent a private jet and pilot to fly them to the beautiful island. She popped a bottle of wine as soon as she got on the plane. "Any last minute words you want to say before we depart Atlanta?" Ty inquired.

"Yes, wake me up when we land." Dom joked.

"No, fareal sweetie. I want you to know that you're the most amazing woman that I could ever ask for. I don't know any woman who would've done what you did for me or who would have been a true rider like you were." Ty looked at Dom with eyes that showed her gratefulness.

"You're forever my lady! Will you marry me?" Dom asked, dropping down on one knee as she pulled out a canary yellow, four-carat, radiant diamond ring. "You wanted to know what took me so long that day I went out to get us something to eat; well, now you see why. I knew you were always going to be my wife, but now I want to make it official; no more playing around, no more outsiders, it's just us—you and me."

Tears came to Ty's eyes when she saw the beautiful diamond ring with the main diamond surrounded by diamonds. She listened to every word that Dom had to say and boy had she waited a long time to hear those words. It was finally real; she belonged to only Dom and Dom belonged only to her.

"Yes, I will marry you." Ty said crying.

Dom slid the ring on Ty's finger. She sat next to her and kissed her tears away. "I love you; you know that right? I always have and I always will."

"I know, I love you too." Ty said as the plane began to take off. Ty sat back and laid her head on Dom's shoulder. She drifted off to sleep with a smile on her face.

~~

The moral to this story is know who you open your life up to. Nowadays everyone has an ulterior motive; your job is to be wise enough to see the person's ulterior motives before it's too late. Benzino, Lorraine and Nasir didn't do that, so it's too late for them; but time is still on your side. Watch the company you keep and the people you fall in love with, whether it be overnight, within a month or a year.

~V. Brown

G STREET CHRONICLES
~ PRESENTS ~

BLACK ICE
SO WE MEET AGAIN

Bonus!
Includes
"Broken Promise"

V. BROWN
THE AUTHOR OF *"BROKEN PROMISE"*

We'd like to thank you for supporting G Street Chronicles and invite you to join our social networks. Please be sure to post a review when you're finished reading.

Facebook
G Street Chronicles Fan Page
G Street Chronicles CEO Exclusive Readers Group

Twitter
@GStreetChronicl

Email us and we'll add you to our mailing list
fans@gstreetchronicles.com

George Sherman Hudson, CEO
Shawna A., COO